The Death of Ivan Ilyich by Leo Tolstoy

Translated by Lynn Solotaroff

With an introduction by Ronald Blythe

BANTAM BOOKS

NEW YORK · TORONTO · LONDON · SYDNEY · AUCKLAND

THE DEATH OF IVAN ILYICH

A Bantam Book
Bantam Classic edition / June 1981

ISBN 0-553-21035-1

Published simultaneously in the United States and Canada

Bantam Books are published by Bantam Books, a division of Bantam Double-day Dell Publishing Group, Inc. Its trademark, consisting of the words "Bantam Books" and the portrayal of a rooster, is Registered in U.S. Patent and Trademark Office and in other countries. Marca Registrada. Bantam Books, 1540 Broadway, New York, New York 10036.

PRINTED IN THE UNITED STATES OF AMERICA

OPM   36   35   34   33   32   31   30   29   28

The Death of
Ivan Ilyich

Introduction

In *The Death of Ivan Ilyich* Tolstoy takes what was for him the tremendous imaginary leap of analyzing the reactions of a man who, until the surprising pain of his terminal illness began, had never given the inevitability of his own dying so much as a passing thought; a man who thus was as unlike Tolstoy as it was possible to be, for Tolstoy was a lifelong deathwatcher. He was, in fact, highly experienced in death and had compulsively observed it from a thousand angles both physically and metaphysically. He could not resist looking at it even when the sight terrified him. Ivan Ilyich, on the other hand, had taken no look and had made no search. Death had announced itself to him in a trivial fashion which, as a worldly careerist, he found idiotic and at first quite unbelievable. He had bumped himself slightly while hanging up draperies; how could such a thing spell annihilation? Was a young-middle-aged high court judge to be swept away by such a trifle? To the judge the notion is as unjust as it is absurd. However, dissolution starts, casually and even delicately at first, then ravenously. One critic of this little novel whose vast theme makes it a masterpiece of literary compression said that instead of descending into the dark places of the soul in this story, Tolstoy "descends with agonizing leisure and precision into the dark places of the body. It is a poem—one of the most harrowing ever conceived—of the insurgent flesh, of the manner in which carnality, with its pains and corruptions, penetrates and dissolves the tenuous discipline of reason."

In a chilling, plain language that has been shorn of most of the descriptive richness of his customary prose style, Tolstoy tells with bleak honesty what it is like to die when the mind is body-bound. He knew what being body-bound meant from his own strenuously earthy instincts, but at least he had developed a spirituality to put these instincts into some kind of focus. But what of a man whose existence had no focus? What happened to him when the little pain that wouldn't go away arrived? And so Tolstoy stares remorselessly through the orifices of the death mask of a man whose social and moral features have nothing whatever in common with his own, a conventional jack-in-office with blunted feelings and a sharp eye for the main chance. That such a person should preside over such a mighty thing as justice only adds to the irony. But we know his type; we see him everywhere still—on the company board as well as on the bench, in politics, advertising and, so far as he can manage it, always in the swim—a tenth-rate exerciser of power over others. Yet Tolstoy raises up this dull and rather despicable man until something about him shines sufficiently for the reader to catch a glimpse of himself reflected in him. He proves how, when it is almost eaten up by disease and frightful to contemplate, and when pain is searching out the breaking point of the intellect, another factor, call it the soul or spirit or the true self, emerges.

The German physician and literary critic A. L. Vischer has investigated the parallel relationship that exists between a man's total personality and his relationship to death. "Simple, uncomplicated souls," he writes, "who do not attach such great importance to their own life, are able to accept their illness, because they accept their fate: life and heart have done their work, time for them to go. By contrast, successful and self-assured people are usually at a complete loss when faced with the reality of physical collapse." And he goes on to describe that popular and macabre theme of the Middle Ages when Death suddenly partners the living in a dance. The beautiful, the young, the important, the rich, the saintly, are each approached "spitefully, brutally, without warning" and are stopped in their tracks. "Today the concept of a blind fate is probably the dominant concept of the first half of life. A man who is in its grip will react by falling back on certain set formulae. He will speak of 'inscrutable ways,' of the 'cruel whims of fate,' i.e., of the all-powerful Moira (the idea of a preordained fate against which it was useless to struggle, and which dominated the death thinking of the ancient Greeks). Such people exist in a perpetual present, their unreflecting lives given over to one long round of activity . . . their unmistakable progress lacks a sense of time." Nearly all this applies to Ivan Ilyich, although Tolstoy's particular difficulty was caused by his long being unable to accept that Death must partner him as it partnered all men. Just how would *he* behave when Death tapped him on the shoulder on some ordinary day when he was decorating a room, making a deal, or blotting a page? He cannot imagine how—it is altogether too impossible and horrible, and this in spite of his Christianity. And so he imagines it happening to a man he could never be—Ivan Ilyich, an opportunistic lawyer with starved emotions and crude vision. Gradually, as disease consumes him, the victim becomes Tolstoy's—and the reader's—spiritual brother and the equal of all humanity, the worst and the best.

The Death of Ivan Ilyich marked the close of Tolstoy's great crisis of faith, which preoccupied him for nearly the whole of the 1870s, and during which the thought that he must die harassed him almost to the point of insanity. The very rationality of death became for him the most irrational thing of all. He could not say, like Michelangelo: "If we have been pleased with life then we should not be displeased with death, since it comes from the hand of the same master," because his entire nature cried out against death as a fact. He felt he could not live if there was death. People have frequently complained of the manner in which death interrupts their work or play: Casanova on his deathbed resented being thrust out of life before the end of the show; and Simone de Beauvoir states that the reason why death fills us with anxiety is that it is the inescapable reversal of our projects. But

Tolstoy's anti-death mania went far beyond such thinking and led him into a labyrinth where, just when by means of some religious or philosophical trick he thought he had shaken off his pursuer, he would turn a corner and meet him face to face. Not Moira, the fate a man had to accept, but the fiend that had to be fought every inch of the way until breath stopped or the heart burst. Ivan Ilyich's terrible screaming resistance to death would have met the approval of Dylan Thomas, who urged his dying father to "rage, rage against the dying of the light," and it forms an unforgettable description of how Tolstoy thought he himself could behave in such a plight. Such resistance is rare. Although the dying are sad about losing out, they are also usually passive. The acceptance of death transforms death, writes Paul-Louis Landsberg in his *Essai sur l'Expérience de la Mort,* which is something neither Tolstoy nor Ivan Ilyich could accept. Both Tolstoy, during the 1870s, and his pathetic hero were like naked victims impotently at the mercy of a fate which their entire instincts fought and denied. Tolstoy, for whom everything that ever happened to him was grist to his literary mill, had to examine this denial of death.

He found a way of doing so after hearing about the death of a provincial judge named Ivan Ilyich Mechnikov. The death had been described to him in some detail by the judge's brother. Mechnikov had presided at the court at Tula, a town near the Tolstoy estate and from whose railway station the writer often watched the victims of Tula justice set out in chains and with shaved heads for Siberia. Count Tolstoy, burning with a Christ-like identification with these poor outcasts, many of them young boys and aged men, had imagined the kind of professional detachment that made it possible for officials like Mechnikov to treat their fellow creatures so inhumanely and then return to dinner with their families and friends. Comforting the prisoners at Tula station, Tolstoy had been amazed by the triviality of their offenses: "One hundred and fourteen persons sent away for failure to possess a passport . . . Two accused of nothing; they're just being deported . . . Two convicts sentenced to hard labor for life, for brawling and manslaughter . . . they were crying. A pleasing face. Appalling stench . . . " he noted. Then suddenly, perhaps one ordinary morning when he was running through the list for the day, Mechnikov himself had been sentenced to the ultimate dark and to the cold—he who had so unfeelingly and for so long doled out death or a half-life to others. What happened inside Mechnikov from then on? At first Tolstoy thought he would set out the effects of this terminal illness in the shape of a diary entitled "The Death of a Judge"; then he changed his mind. His own death fears had to be incorporated in this book, because the chief reason why we can tolerate death in others, even in those near to us, is that it pushes it away from ourselves. In this story Tolstoy would join a man in his death to the limits of his literary power. "Take the saving lie from the average man and you take his happiness away," said Ibsen. The biggest saving lie is to accept a friend's death and not one's own.

Tolstoy was highly experienced in death, and from childhood onward his diaries, letters, and books reveal how much it intrigued him. His death "notes" range from the detailed studies he made of slaughter on the battlefield to an execution in Paris, from the animallike acceptance of death by the muzhiks on his estates to the greatly varying reactions he had to the many deaths in his own family. These, as was customary at all times until our own, included the frequent deaths of children. Sometimes he showed uncontrollable grief over the death of one of his little boys, sometimes almost a callousness, as though he was keeping death in its place. He was fascinated to discover that death annoyed him as much as it saddened him, and in the *The Death of Ivan Ilyich* there is a lot of plain, ordinary irritation floating around. Neither the dying man nor those attending him have any time for death, and they are vexed when they are forced to give it their full attention.

Tolstoy was remembering how put out he had been when his brother Dmitry died and how, in his youthful defiance of the etiquette of bereavement, he had behaved very badly. Yet he had not been able to stop himself. When he had come to his brother's sickroom and seen this terrible object with "his enormous wrist as though soldered to the bones of his forearm," he felt that what he was seeing was no more than a miserable, useless part of himself, and so he

7

freed himself from it with what he considered then was a natural revulsion. This brother's life, brief though it was, had been Tolstoy's spiritual journey in reverse. First of all Dmitry had been extravagantly chaste and pure, and then, at twenty-six, he had plunged into debauchery. So total had been his sensuality, in fact, that, rather like Genet, he had transformed it into a sacrament. Tolstoy, staring at him before he hurried away, saw that "his face had been devoured by his eyes." Later, picking away at his motives for deserting his brother, he writes: "I felt sorry for Mitya (Dmitry) but not very. . . . I honestly believe that what bothered me most about his death was that it prevented me from attending a performance at Court to which I had been invited." In Jane Austen's *Mansfield Park* a young man is furious when a play he is about to take part in is canceled because of the death of a grandmother, and in Proust's novel, the Duc de Guermantes pretends that news of a death hasn't reached him so that he can attend a party. Mourning customs in the West have been reduced to the minimum in order that "life may go on." Religious people will talk glibly of their belief in resurrection to excuse this disregard, but as Paul Tournier, a real Christian, observes: "Resurrection does not do away with death. It follows it. I cannot minimize death because I believe in resurrection."

With all but two exceptions, those surrounding Ivan Ilyich at his end feel sorry for him, "but not very." Sorrow is a formality and he himself knows it. Nearly everything in his life has been a formality—his outlook, his marriage, his work, and his hopes—and he is hurt but not surprised by the conventional reaction to his tragedy. When his colleagues first heard the news, "the death of a close acquaintance evoked in them all the usual feeling of relief that it was someone else, not they, who had died. 'Well, isn't that something—he's dead, but I'm not.'" And then the tedious demands of propriety, as Tolstoy calls them, have to be obeyed, and all the familiar protective rituals set in motion, not so much for the dear departed as for the safety of his friends. Have they not been grimly dragged away from food and money, cards and conversation, power and ambition, to the dull house of the dead? No small part of Ivan Ilyich's suffering is caused by his understanding of all this. He knows, for instance, that he is no longer the head of the house but an obstacle to his family, "and that his wife had adopted a certain attitude toward his illness and clung to it regardless of what he said or did." In one of the novel's poignant moments, the sheer desolating aloneness of dying is evoked when, "after supper his friends went home, leaving Ivan Ilyich alone with the knowledge that his life had been poisoned and was poisoning the life of others. . . . He had to go on living like this, on the brink of disaster, without a single person to understand and pity him."

It is death as it is watched by the dying that Tolstoy probes here. Death as it is glimpsed by the healthy or imaginatively understood by the artistic is not his theme. Neither is it death as seen by doctors, for these he despises. What he concentrates on is the plight of a man who has a coldly adequate language for dealing with another's death but who remains incoherent when it comes to his own. When death actually begins to happen, when one has to say, like Ivan Ilyich, that "it's not a question of a caecum or a kidney, but of life and . . . death. Yes, life was there and now it's going, going . . ."—what then? What words? What useful clichés even? What soothing talk about us all having to go sometime? That remarkable though neglected novelist John Cowper Powys once gave the bitter answer in these words:

"He it is who—and make no mistake, my friend, the poor devil is yourself—who now, very now, visualizes the inflamed condition of his prostate gland in the curves of the pattern on his lavatory floor. There is the appalling possibility that the 'I' upon whom this whole world of intimate impressions depends will soon have to face its absolute *annihilation*. The sun will rise as before, and the winds will blow as before. People will talk of the weather in the same tone. The postman will knock as he did just now and the letters will fall on the mat. But *he* won't be there. He, our pivot and the center of everything, will be nowhere at all." In *The Death of Ivan Ilyich* Tolstoy puts the same realization thus: " 'Yes, life was there and now it's going, going, and I can't hold on to it. Yes. Why deceive myself? Isn't it clear to everyone but me that I'm dying, that it's only a question of weeks, days—perhaps minutes? Before there was light, now there is darkness. Before I was here, now I am going there. Where?' He broke out in a cold sweat, his breathing died down. All he could hear was the beating of his heart. 'I'll be gone. What will there be then? Nothing. So where will I be when I'm gone?'"

Maurice Maeterlinck, the Belgian poet who was born a generation later than Tolstoy and who lived long enough to see the holocaust of both world wars, often attacked the convention by which we allow a whole range of expressions for dealing with the deaths of strangers, neighbors, friends, parents—even our children and lovers—but almost none at all for the death which must come to ourselves. When Ivan Ilyich realized that he was lost, that there was no return, "that the end had come, the very end," he didn't use words at all but began three days of incessant screaming. He screamed with an "O" sound, writes Tolstoy. It reminds us of Edvard Munch's famous work "The Scream," painted in 1893, and which has been described as a John-the-Baptist-like cry to an unprepared world, to unmindful minds. The totally alone figures in the paintings of Francis Bacon also echo this solitary noise which is both protest and prophecy.

Earlier in his mortal illness Ivan Ilyich had "cried about his helplessness, about his terrible loneliness, about the cruelty of people, about the cruelty of God, about the absence of God," about once articulate concepts and ideas which were now letting him down. Although bitter and indignant, like a little boy in his tears and rage, he yet retained the belief that one or all of these temporarily unkind forces would stop hounding him, that they would even show him their benign side and comfort him and kiss him better. The nightmare would pass because, up until now, nightmares had always passed. Then there returns the plain black fact: He is dying. Ironically, he can only attract the attention of his friends and of his God by acknowledging this. But acknowledgment is horrifying, and thus the adult screaming, the most dreadful of all sounds.

Maeterlinck was amazed by the crudeness of Western man's thought when it came to the subject of his own death. The fatuity and shallowness of man's philosophy appalled him. "We deliver death into the dim hands of instinct," he writes in *La Morte*, "and we grant it not one hour of our intelligence. Is it surprising that the idea of death, which should be the most perfect and the most luminous, remains the flimsiest of our ideas and the only one that is backward? How should we know the one power we never look in the face? To fathom its abysses we wait until the most enfeebled, the most disordered moments of our life arrive." Ivan Ilyich certainly does this, and Tolstoy even goes so far as to create in the dying judge a hint of actual frustration when, his screaming done and his hour come, it occurs to him that now he won't have time to explore the fascinatingly interesting and no longer hideous territory of his own death. Yet only an hour before this intellectual peace descends, Ivan Ilyich is experiencing the peak of terror as he finds himself in the conflict of appearing to be thrust into a black hole and, at the same time, not able to be engulfed in it.

"What prevented him from getting into it was the belief that his life had been a good one. This justification of his life held him fast, kept him from moving forward, and caused him more agony than anything else. Suddenly some force struck him in the chest and the side and made his breathing even more constricted: he plunged into the hole and there, at the bottom, something was shining. What had happened to him was what one frequently experiences in a railway car when one thinks one is going forward, but is actually moving backward, and suddenly becomes aware of the actual direction. 'Yes, all of it was simply *not the real thing*. But no matter. I can still make it *the real thing*—I can. But what *is* the real thing?' Ivan Ilyich asked himself . . ."

The real thing involves a recognition of death as a natural corollary of life. It is no good being platitudinous about it, or brave and witty like Epicurus who said: "How should I fear death? When I am, death is not; and when death is, I am not." Neither will the steadily increasing application of modern hygienics make it disappear, like a stubborn stain under a detergent. Present trends are to make us conscious of death as a mass social tragedy which, by means of compassion, economics, improved medicine, and the like, can be conquered. Multiple death in wars, famines, epidemics, accidents—even as a statistic issued by the anti-smoke and drink lobbies—is shown as not incurable, and talk of this death sends no shiver down the individual spine. But

private death, individual death, one's own death—
that is quite another matter. The language for
this has become repressive and full of clinical
taboos. There were some who preferred this slur-
ring and dimming of the eloquence of death even
during the century when Tolstoy was writing.
Napoleon complained that "the doctors and the
priests have long been making death grievous."
For the professional slayer, it was clearly nothing
much to grieve about. We too are anxious to play
the whole subject down and discourage morbid-
ity. It's all best left unsaid, unfelt now for as
long as possible, and, with the help of last-min-
ute drugs, forever, if we are lucky. Don't look,
it is death, is what we are told now. Call in the
people who deal with that kind of thing; there
will be terminal and disposal problems. Best
leave it to the experts.

Yet nature, art, religion, literature—all the
great progenitors of our living awareness—tell
us that death is a positive and quite individual
occurrence, and that to refuse to look at it is the
most certain way of shrinking our responses to
everything else. "Be absolute for death," insisted
Shakespeare, adding that by doing so we will
make life as well as death the sweeter. And
George Herbert, writing during the seventeenth
century when our own scientific society was
emerging, could say, without any of the revulsion which overtook Ivan Ilyich when he discovered "that horrid, appalling, unheard-of
something that had been set in motion within
him," that he felt death was at work within him
"like a mole." Maeterlinck endorses this accep-

tance. It is not the arrival of death but life that we must act upon, he says. "Evil rises up from every side at the approach of death, but not at its call; and though they gather round it, they did not come with it. . . . We impute to it the tortures of the last illness . . . but illnesses have nothing in common with that which ends them. They form part of life, and not of death. We easily forget the most cruel sufferings . . . and the first sign of convalescence destroys the most unbearable memories of the room of pain. But let death come, and at once we overwhelm it with all the evil done before it. Not a tear but is remembered as a reproach, not a cry of pain but it becomes a cry of accusation." Death for Ivan Ilyich is his cancer right up until the penultimate moment of his life when, briefly and tantalizingly, he perceives something altogether different and entirely acceptable. The Christian-scientific philosopher Teilhard de Chardin prayed that he might have an understanding of the terminal process when God was painfully parting the fibers of his being in order to penetrate to the marrow of his substance and bear him away within Himself. Tolstoy's own egotism made it impossible for him to accept death in these passive, mystical terms, and Ivan Ilyich's dreadful struggles are an honest description of how Tolstoy thought he himself might have behaved in similar circumstances.

Acceptance of death when it arrives is one thing, but to allow it to upstage the joys of living is ingratitude. Ivan Ilyich's gray tragedy is that of a man who debased life and who tried to fight off death. Tolstoy presents the judge's life in coldly accurate terms which might almost be a summary heard in his own court. It is shot through with accusation. What did you do with this divine asset, Life? demands Tolstoy. You made no attempt to live it outside the meanest terms. You played safe according to the most selfish rules. You took care to see that everything you did was done with "clean hands, in clean shirts, and with French phrases." You never put a foot wrong and so you never stepped out of your rut. Your life has been "most simple and commonplace—and most horrifying." The bleak indictment continues with Ivan Ilyich's opportunism, marriage of convenience, vanity, and limitation, and then, with astonishment, the reader finds himself beginning to like this conventional man and to be sorry when he starts to lose out to death.

In sympathizing with the judge, cut off in his prime, as he thought, although the average expectation of life for a man in the 1880s was forty-one years, we are sympathizing with ourselves and all the little hopes and aspirations we have; aspirations which are so despicable or laughable when put into our dossier or official record but which are so precious to us. Ivan Ilyich's death remains one of the most self-identifying deaths in all literature; his death in life, his death as transient flesh, they are still visibly exact reflections of our own deathliness. Although it is nearly a century since Tolstoy wrote this brilliant story, we read it without detachment. It is not a period piece except in such things as comparative terminal nursing. That screaming might be tranquilized today, but not the death ignorance which caused it. Above all the gulf dividing the dying from the living is no less now than when Ivan Ilyich sees that "the awesome, terrifying act of his dying had been degraded by those about him to the level of a chance unpleasantness, a bit of unseemly behavior (they reacted to him as they would to a man who emitted a foul odor on entering a drawing room); that it had been degraded by that very 'propriety' to which he had devoted his entire life." We too play death down when it is happening and, later, simply clean it up, pushing its profundity out of sight.

Tolstoy was fifty-seven when he published *The Death of Ivan Ilyich*. Since the wild success of *Anna Karenina*, which had come out in installments between 1875–77 and in book form in 1878, he had been caught up in what his wife called "a disease," an experiment in living according to the actual rules laid down by Christ and his followers—a faith he believed had quite disappeared under centuries of myth, politics, the orthodoxy of religious institutions, and mere social convenience. It was an experiment that was eventually to lead him to excommunication as well as to the meaning of death, pain, and the conflict between loving life and having to accept that it was temporal. "Leo is still working," wrote his wife to her sister, "but, alas, all he is producing are philosophical disquisitions! He reads and writes until it gives him a headache. And all in order to prove that the Church does not accord with the Gospels. There are not ten people in Russia who can be interested in such a subject. But there's nothing to be done. My only hope is that he will soon get over it." She was only partly relieved when she heard that he had begun a story called "The Death of a Judge" because during the years since he had worked regularly as a novelist, attempts at fiction had come to nothing. However, when the long short story, now entitled *The Death of Ivan Ilyich*, appeared, all Countess Tolstoy's faith in her husband as a writer of genius returned.

Although from this point on he would let his imagination, and not religious and political theories alone, dictate his work, becoming again the great artist he had been, these years marked an estrangement between Tolstoy and his Countess. They would end in his flight from her and his quite impossible-to-imagine death in the station master's cottage at Astapovo, surrounded by the first mass-media publicity machinery of the twentieth century. News of his dying had spread across the world, and immense crowds controlled by police and the militia attended his end. Barred from his bedside, his wife's flattened face stared through the window until someone hung a blanket up to prevent their eyes meeting. Here the similarity to the stress between Ivan Ilyich and his wife is prophetic. The Countess's adoration of the genius who had abandoned her was neurotic but total; but Ivan Ilyich knows that his wife doesn't love him and so can't go very far with him along the black road that stretches ahead. Only near the end, as death acceptance creates understanding and forgiveness, does he come close to her, but until then "he hates her with every inch of his being." Tolstoy too died with difficulty. His disciples, the "Tolstoyens," heard his last words: "The truth . . . I care a great deal . . . How they . . ." But in spite of a solemn promise to ask him about death as it occurred, they said nothing themselves. Tolstoy said that when he was dying they were to ask him if he saw life as he usually saw it, or whether he saw it as a progression toward love and God. "If I should not have the strength to speak, and the answer is yes, I shall close my eyes; if it is no, I shall look up." But none of them troubled him with this question. The dying are in the hands of the living, who generally remain more loyal to deathbed conveniences than to deathbed revelations. It comforts them to know that the dead knew and felt nothing. "He felt nothing," they will later tell each other, forgetting that there are more things to feel than pain and fear. Yet men have always thought of a conscious death as their mortal birthright and have prayed that they "would not die as the unconscious things, the frozen sparrow under the hedge, the dead leaf whirled away before the night wind . . ." But we, confronted by a glimpse of infinity and threatened by last words, cling fast to clichés and analgesics. Feel nothing, say nothing, see nothing, we advise the dying while smoothing the rubber sheet and administering the drug.

In the West, twentieth century habits surrounding our entering and leaving the world are determined by these exits and entrances no longer taking place in the home but in the hospital. When children were born and parents died in the actual marriage bed, where first and last cries were heard in the very same room, where the first things looked at were often the last things seen, where the corpse lay where the lover's body moved, when the entire intimacy of life from start to finish was confined to the family house and not to maternity wings, terminal wards and funeral parlors, death itself possessed dimensions and connotations that are now either forgotten or stifled. Everyone until recently knew the actual smell of death. In a big family during the nineteenth century, it was not unusual for it to be an annual smell and to take its position in the odorous year along with springtime beeswaxings, summer jams, and winter fires. When death came, it was the family who dealt with it, not the specialists. Death's mysteries and its chores became inseparable.

Tolstoy wrote through, as it were, numerous family deaths, and he lost one small son while actually at work on *Ivan Ilyich*. His reactions to these periodic losses fluctuated wildly from desolation and horror to a coldly grandiloquent form of acceptance. He either went to pieces over a bereavement or became unfeelingly heroic. On one occasion in 1873 when his little son Petya died, he actually panicked and fled from his house to Moscow because he thought he might catch death as one caught an infection. Yet, sometime later, when the four-year-old Alexis followed his brothers to the grave in one of those repetitive little processions which formerly regulated parenthood, Tolstoy found a quite different way of stepping out of death's path, this time by applying hard logic. "All I can say is that the death of a child, which I once thought incomprehensible and unjust, now seems reasonable and good . . . My wife has been much afflicted by this death and I, too, am sorry that the little boy I loved is no longer here, but despair is only for those who shut their eyes to the commandment by which we are ruled." Quite the worst period for him for dealing with death were the years 1873–75, when he lost three children and two adored aunts.

"It is time to die," he wrote somberly. "That is not true. What *is* true is there is nothing else to do in life but die. I feel it every instant. I am writing, I'm working hard . . . but there is no happiness for me in any of it," he told his brother. "Every minor illness, every death among his acquaintances, brought him back to the thought of his own end," writes his biographer Henri Troyat, describing the time when Tolstoy's fame as a novelist and his powers as an artist soared in reverse ratio to his confidence in staying alive. "Why was fate dogging his heels like this? He felt as though he were skirmishing with some animal—intelligent, powerful, and vindictive—that had been trained to snap at him. In a moment of abject anxiety he wrote to a friend, 'Fear, horror, death, the children laughing and gay. Special food, agitation, doctors, lies, death, horror—it was torture!' *Death was* and yet he had to stay sane and work and earn money and look forward to Easter and cut the hay. . . .

"One strange thing in both *Anna Karenina* and *War and Peace*," says Troyat, "it is the exceptional, glittering beings, those marked by some metaphysical sign, who disappear, and the average, even insignificant ones who survive and trudge along their little paths, halfway between good and evil." Ivan Ilyich is the exception. Here it is meanness of spirit which is made to produce its own pathos. Against every inclination we find ourselves sorrowing for a man for whom we have no natural sympathy. The traditions governing death in nineteenth century fiction are broken page by page. This is how it really happens, Tolstoy is saying, this is what the outrage of the ego is like.

The novel is masterly in its brevity and in the use made of dramatic foreshortening. The reader rapidly finds out that he lacks all the usual perspectives for looking at the familiar nineteenth century deathbed scene and that he is at once plunged into realities concerning himself. He is forced to look down to a ledge where a man clings without dignity and out of reach of help. Above the man, only just beyond his grasp, stands everything that once held him safe and sound: home, job, and society. Below him lies a spinning darkness. Agony is created by those above accepting the situation, by even being rational about it. A nonidentifying process has moved across their usual view of him like a filter, and already, with the breath still in him, he is outside their comprehension. One of Tolstoy's themes is about the inability of the dying to communicate and of the sick to remain inside the old circle of relationships. The very first hint that Ivan Ilyich is poorly begins the pushing-out business, as wife, children, and colleagues prepare to live in a world that will no longer contain him. Self-interest reigns. Gain runs parallel with loss. It is a busy period for everyone and there really isn't much time for being sad. Afterward, when he has slipped from the ledge and out of sight, empty words are politely muttered in the empty space he has left. There is coarse honesty when the dead man's friend takes the opportunity to set up a game of whist while viewing the corpse. The widow acts out the grief she is supposed to feel and receives the condolences of those who are not sorry. It is finished—a life that proved to have no meaning for anyone except he who possessed it and who parted with it with fear and incredulity.

Ivan Ilyich is the climax of Tolstoy's death writing. It also acted as the purgative to his own extreme death fears which reached their crescendo during a visit he made to the town of Arzamas. The incident is crucial to Tolstoy's obsessional fascination with death in all its variety. Shortly after the publication of *War and Peace*, when his body had never felt more vigorous or his mind more active, with praise and success ringing in his ears, and when his life should have been bursting with a sense of well-being, he fell into a deep despair that took the form of being irreconcilably opposed to the inevitability of his own death. His biographer Henri

23

Troyat has described Tolstoy's fear as animal, visceral, chilling. "It came on him all of a sudden—he began to tremble, sweat broke out on his forehead, he felt a presence behind his back. Then the jaws of the vise loosened, the shadow passed on, life tumbled in upon him, the tiniest vein in his body rejoiced at the surge of new blood," and he felt safe. But only temporarily. So he plunged into activities he hoped would be a hedge against death—ordinary, practical, earthy matters, such as extending his estate with the royalties from *War and Peace*. There was land for sale hundreds of miles away from Yasnaya Polyana, his ancestral home, and so he traveled there with a servant of whom he was particularly fond, a laughing, high-spirited boy named Sergey. It was not Count Tolstoy the saint but Count Tolstoy the capitalist on this opportunist jaunt: "I was looking for a seller who was an imbecile with no business sense and it seemed to me that I had found one."

The trip began happily enough, then the frightfulness started to return, dogging his footsteps, catching up with him just when Sergey's cheerfulness and goodness promised protection. Saying nothing to the boy, Tolstoy took a room at the inn at Arzamas, and there the classic existentialist nightmare overwhelmed him. The room was death and he was in it. "I was particularly disturbed by the fact that it was square," he wrote. It was full of torment and the torment was irrevocable. What was in the room with him *had to be*—this was the delirium of it. There *was* no escape, no way out—or in, if it came to that. He was. Death was. "Where am I? Where am I going? What am I running away from?" he thought—a thought which he never allowed Ivan Ilyich. Later, in a short story called *Notes of a Madman*, Tolstoy set out the whole terrible experience.

"'This is ridiculous,' I told myself. 'Why am I so depressed? What am I afraid of?'

"'Of me,' answered Death. 'I am here.'

"A cold shudder ran over my skin. Yes, Death. It will come, it is already here, even though it has nothing to do with me now . . . My whole being ached with the need to live, the right to live, and, at the same moment, I felt death at work. And it was awful being torn apart inside. I tried to shake off my terror. I found the stump of a candle in a brass candlestick and lighted it. The reddish flame, the candle, the candlestick, all told me the same story: there is nothing in life, nothing exists but death, and death should not be!"

The "square white and red horror" Tolstoy found himself in was his tomb. All rooms were tombs. All talk was part of the everlasting silence, all movement no more than a slight twitching of the thick stillness, all horizons but walls. This was the shattering message of Arzamas. Soon after turning it into *Notes of a Madman* Tolstoy began to apply his death findings to his neighbor Judge Mechnikov, the sort of person he could never be, turning him into a man who knew nothing about rooms being tombs until an errant window knob prodded him to draw his attention to the fact.

The two major Existentialists, Jean-Paul Sartre and Martin Heidegger, take conflicting views of Tolstoy's room. For Heidegger it is an anti-room, stark and dreadful certainly, but leading on to what we are too mortal to imagine, though not black and destructive. For Sartre (who confessed that the idea of death haunted him during his childhood because he did not love life), death is simply a hard fact like birth. "It is absurd that we should be born, it is absurd that we shall die . . . Life, so long as it lasts, is pure and free of any death. For I can conceive of myself only as alive. Man is a being for life, not for death." Heidegger takes the opposite view. "Death is not an event which happens to man, but an event which he lives through from birth onwards. . . . As soon as man lives he is old enough to die . . . Death is a constituent of our being. Day after day we live through death. Man is, in his essence, a being for death. What is the meaning of this death for the individual consciousness? That by interrupting life it makes it complete. Incompletion is a constituent of my being . . . Death teaches us that life is a value, but an incomplete value." While on the road to Arzamas, Tolstoy was telling himself that life should be pure and free of any death; thirteen years later, nervously yet compulsively, like someone tonguing a jumpy nerve in a tooth, he is exploring Heidegger's notion of life as an incomplete value and forcing Ivan Ilyich to accept that, at forty-five, he was old enough to die and that he was, and always had been, a being for death.

Finally, we must say something about the last illness which, in Ivan Ilyich's case, was also the first illness, for the story is as much a morality of the sickroom as of the grave. In his memoir *Confession*, written the same year he began *The Death of Ivan Ilyich*, Tolstoy relates an old Easter fable which for him is about a man desperately clinging to life while cancer eats away inside him. It is the allegorical version of Ivan Ilyich's fate.

"There is an Easter fable, told a long time ago, about a traveler caught in open country by a wild beast. To escape from the beast the traveler jumps into a dry well, but at the bottom of the well he sees a dragon with its jaws open to devour him. And the unfortunate man, not daring to climb out lest he be destroyed by the wild beast, and not daring to jump to the bottom of the well lest he be devoured by the dragon, seizes hold of a branch of a wild bush growing in a crack in the well and clings to it. His arms grow weaker and weaker, and he feels he will soon have to abandon himself to the destruction which awaits him above or below; but still he clings on and as he clings on he looks around and he sees that two mice, one black and one white, are steadily circling round the branch of the bush he is hanging on, and gnawing at it. Soon it will snap and break off, and he will fall into the dragon's jaws.

"The traveler sees this and knows that he will inevitably perish; but while he hangs on he looks around and finds some drops of honey on the leaves of the bush, reaches them with his tongue and licks them.

"So I too clung to the branches of life, knowing that the dragon death was inevitably waiting for me, ready to tear me to pieces, and I could not understand why this agony had befallen me. And I tried to lick the honey which had previously consoled me, but the honey no longer gave me pleasure, while the black and white mice, day and night, gnawed the branch I was clinging to. . . . I could not tear my gaze from them. No matter how often I was told: 'You cannot understand the meaning of life, so do not think about it, but live,' I could not do it because I had done it for too long. I could not help now seeing that day and night running around bringing me nearer to death. That is all I could see, because only that is the truth. All the rest is lies. . . ."

For Tolstoy the black and white mice were the scuttling days and nights hastening him to the tomb; for Ivan Ilyich the disease eating its way through his body. Tolstoy despaired at the time because "the two drops of honey," which were his family and his writing, failed to console him about death. But what of a man who lacked any true sweetness in his life when death preoccupied him, and who thought, not in the manner in which a healthy person thinks, of the years passing and what can he do about it, but as someone incurably ill thinks. The brilliance of the book lies not in yet another of Tolstoy's vivid deathbed scenes, but in this solitary thinking of its occupant as he is driven by pain and weakness toward—what? It is the tragedy of a man who is a death illiterate and who has to make his way out of the world through the ranks of other death illiterates. They degrade his passage and fill it with vulgarities. They do what they understand is necessary, and for Ivan Ilyich it is all play-acting and unnecessary. He sees that when a man is made disgusting through sickness, all those people with whom he has made his life become disgusting as well. And just as he made others suffer and cringe by exercising the law in a professionally obscure manner which made them powerless, he sees that the doctors are doing the very same kind of thing to him. Men make money and reputation by joining one or other of "the conspiracy of clerks."

Real help, if not salvation, comes from the lowly. When Tolstoy had been so miserable and frightened at Arzamas, his instinct had been to find the optimistic Sergey in the hope that the young servant's joyful nature would blot out his nightmare. But the boy was asleep and Tolstoy had felt vulnerable and forsaken in his Gethsemane. In *The Death of Ivan Ilyich* he makes the reverse happen. A pantry boy named Gerasim, simple, kind, and blooming with health, nurses his master with the most disinterested love for a fellow human being, carrying out the most sordid tasks with complete naturalness. He is neither scared of death nor self-consciously glad to be alive. He finds nothing incongruous in the contact between his beautiful body and the filth of the sick man. Soon Gerasim becomes for Ivan

Ilyich the only decency left. He lies with his legs up on the boy's shoulders, drawing ease from him. In some of Tolstoy's most moving passages we watch this last friendship expand as the judge realizes that what Gerasim gives him comes from free will and selflessness and lies outside anything he could command. Gerasim is loving about life but pragmatic about death and everything connected with the breakdown of physical functioning which precedes it. "'We all have to die someday,'" he says, "displaying an even row of healthy white peasant teeth." And yet it was Gerasim who "was the only one who understood and pitied him." The dying ache for pity, yet the living for some reason find it hard to give real, genuine pity. The idea of Gerasim the simple man helping the spiritual cripple from a more sophisticated society to die is an old one. His most recent appearance was in Pasolini's film *Theorem*, an appearance, one should add, which Tolstoy would have found too explicit as well as blasphemous. For here it must be said that Tolstoy's dilemma over the problem of death was a Christian one. His preoccupation with the subject eventually became rather distasteful to some of his contemporaries, Gorky in particular. Christ-like he may be, declared Gorky the Marxist, but Christ-like in the sense of vanquishing death he is not, nor ever could be. "Although I admire him, I do not like him. . . . He is exaggeratedly preoccupied, he sees nothing and knows nothing outside himself. . . . He lowers himself in my eyes by his fear of death and his pitiful flirtation with it; as a rabid individualist, it gives him a sort of illusion of immortality."

Tolstoy was in his early seventies when this indictment was made. But his recurring death inquiry was not egotistical; it was made on the battlefield, on the scaffold, in the nursery, in the peasant's hut, in palaces, in gutters, everywhere he witnessed the silencing of the marvelous physical machine. It is an inquiry we all make, one way or another. Death astounds us, and the inexorable movement toward it, once it starts, shocks us. Most of us do not see it as a crisis of growth, like Cardinal Danielou, but as the unmentionable odor of decomposition which the shifty mourners in Ivan Ilyich's house watch Gerasim smothering with carbolic. Generally, like the sentenced judge, we draw our conclusions from the certainty of the deaths of friends and strangers, and not of ourselves. The latter is too weird an operation, like arranging mirrors to catch our profile.

Because the dead are bad company, and faith has failed to convince us otherwise, we pray against death, fervently, madly, like the character in Peguy's *Joan of Arc*. "To pray. To pray that a whole people be spared from falling among the dead souls, the dead peoples, the dead nations. Be spared from falling down dead. Be spared from becoming a dead people, a dead nation. Be spared from mildew. Be spared from going rotten in spiritual death, in the earth, in hell . . ." This was how Tolstoy prayed at Arzamas (though using the Our Father). This was what Ivan Ilyich was praying when he screamed for three whole days. But no man is spared death. Tolstoy's ceaseless toiling after the truth in depth had to involve the dead, and this involvement had to bring him—sensual, thriving, vital, and intellectually dazzling seeker after light though he was—to the swirling abyss and into the fears of those sliding into it. Blind fate (Moira) or that intimate transition of the spirit of the loving Creator? Tolstoy dearly longed to know. In *The Death of Ivan Ilyich* he took a man to the brink of having to leave the world much as he had entered it, kicking and screaming, because he had not taken the trouble to grow up, morally speaking, while he was passing through it, and had then shown how salvation could overtake a slowing pulse rate, bringing maturity at the last.

Love masters death at the penultimate hour in Tolstoy's story. It could have rescued Ivan Ilyich from all the fright and despair which terrorized him during the final two weeks had he allowed it to. But so rigidly had he repressed love throughout his adult life that anything pointing to its enduring nature, such as certain happy memories of his childhood, upset him. At some early moment in his development he had taken a stand against love and all that emanated from it, but which he now saw as "the real thing," and had cynically opted for other values, although exactly why he had done this he could not say. He just had. Realizing this during his illness had produced a spiritual anguish which even exceeded his physical agony. During these double sufferings, sights and touches, not language, began to reduce everything that had created this base self with its smart life-style to worthless rubble. The first sight was of the disinterested goodness in his servant boy's face and the first touch was of Gerasim's strength so lovingly put at his service.

The lawyer in Ivan Ilyich immediately put up a case for the defense of the values upon which he constructed his life, only to discover that "there was nothing left to defend." His eyes were then opened to a "dreadful, enormous deception that shut out both life and death." His wife, whom he now views as a leading force in the notions that have been dragging him to damnation, persuades him to admit that taking the sacrament has made him feel better, and in revulsion he shouts at her: "Leave me alone."

Yet belatedly and briefly in their dreary marriage, she is offering him her sensitivity and love. But as with those pure recollections of love in boyhood, he cannot bear "the real thing" from her. Not now, not at this stage. And so, isolated because he is convinced that the strength of love such as that which Gerasim personifies cannot reach him, and quite skeptical of there being such a thing as love in the fake world of himself and his wife, the sick judge is convinced that he can neither go forward or backward in terms of spiritual growth, and that "he was lost." It is a ghastly conviction causing him to scream, first "Oh! No!" and then simply a perpetual, hollow "O."

And it is into this vacuum of horror that love enters without words. Ivan Ilyich's delirious hand comes into chance contact with the head of his son. The boy has stolen into the awful room, and as he feels his father's hand on his hair, seizes and kisses it. Looking up, Ivan Ilyich sees that his wife is also in the room and that unwiped tears are running down her nose. Thus, unlike Tolstoy's death room at Arzamas, this room in which Ivan Ilyich is about to spend his last hour on earth *does* contain love, "and suddenly it became clear to him that what had been oppressing him and would not leave him suddenly was vanishing all at once—from two sides, ten sides, all sides. . . . 'So that's it,'" he told himself just before an even greater recognition arrived with his stopped breath.

As one of the major death explorations in literature, this story has fascinated and influenced many novelists. Its ideas can be traced in I. A. Bunin's *The Gentleman from San Francisco* and in Arthur Miller's *Death of a Salesman*, and parallels have been drawn between the fate of Ivan Ilyich and Kafka's Joseph K. in *The Trial*. Gorky too went to this overwhelming narrative for the theme of his play *Yegor Bulychov and the Others*. But the finest bringing together of all the novel's disturbing themes of vainglory, temporary authority, pain, disease, marital disgust, innocence, and mortality has been the achievement of Alexander Solzhenitsyn in his *Cancer Ward*, where Rusanov, the petty official, abruptly finds his well-ordered life "on the *other* side of his tumor."

Ronald Blythe

The Death of Ivan Ilyich

Chapter 1

In the large building housing the Law Courts, during a recess in the Melvinsky proceedings, members of the court and the public prosecutor met in the office of Ivan Egorovich Shebek, where the conversation turned on the celebrated Krasov case. Fyodor Vasilyevich vehemently denied that it was subject to their jurisdiction, Ivan Egorovich clung to his own view, while Pyotr Ivanovich, who had taken no part in the dispute from the outset, glanced through a copy of the *News* that had just been delivered.

"Gentlemen!" he said. "Ivan Ilyich is dead."

"Really?"

"Here, read this," he said to Fyodor Vasilyevich, handing him the fresh issue, still smelling of printer's ink.

Framed in black was the following announcement: "With profound sorrow Praskovya Fyodorovna Golovina informs relatives and acquaintances that her beloved husband, Ivan Ilyich Golovin, Member of the Court of Justice, passed away on the 4th of February, 1882. The funeral will be held on Friday at one o'clock."

Ivan Ilyich had been a colleague of the gentlemen assembled here and they had all been fond of him. He had been ill for some weeks and his disease was said to be incurable. His post had been kept open for him, but it had been speculated that in the event of his death Alekseev might be appointed to his place and either Vinnikov or Shtabel succeed Alekseev. And so the first thought that occurred to each of the gentlemen in this office, learning of Ivan Ilyich's death, was what effect it would have on their own transfers and promotions or those of their acquaintances.

"Now I'm sure to get Shtabel's post or Vinnikov's," thought Fyodor Vasilyevich. "It was promised to me long ago, and the promotion will mean an increase of eight hundred rubles in salary plus an allowance for office expenses."

"I must put in a request to have my brother-in-law transferred from Kaluga," thought Pyotr Ivanovich. "My wife will be very happy. Now she won't be able to say I never do anything for her family."

"I had a feeling he'd never get over it," said Pyotr Ivanovich. "Sad."

"What, exactly, was the matter with him?"

"The doctors couldn't decide. That is, they decided, but in different ways. When I last saw him, I thought he would recover."

"And I haven't been there since the holidays. I kept meaning to go."

"Was he a man of any means?"

"His wife has a little something, I think, but nothing much."

"Well, there's no question but that we'll have to go and see her. They live so terribly far away."

"From you, that is. From your place, everything's far away."

"You see, he just can't forgive me for living on the other side of the river," said Pyotr Ivanovich, smiling at Shebek. And with that they began talking about relative distances in town and went back to the courtroom.

In addition to the speculations aroused in each man's mind about the transfers and likely job changes this death might occasion, the very fact of the death of a close acquaintance evoked in them all the usual feeling of relief that it was someone else, not they, who had died.

"Well, isn't that something—he's dead, but I'm not," was what each of them thought or felt. The closer acquaintances, the so-called friends of Ivan Ilyich, involuntarily added to themselves that now they had to fulfill the tedious demands of propriety by attending the funeral service and paying the widow a condolence call.

Fyodor Vasilyevich and Pyotr Ivanovich had been closest to him. Pyotr Ivanovich had studied law with Ivan Ilyich and considered himself indebted to him. At dinner that evening he told his wife the news of Ivan Ilyich's death, conjectured about the possibility of having her brother transferred to their district, and then, dispensing with his usual nap, he put on a dress coat and drove to Ivan Ilyich's home.

A carriage and two cabs were parked before the entrance. Downstairs in the hallway, next to the coat stand, a coffin lid decorated with silk brocade, tassels, and highly polished gilt braid was propped against the wall. Two women in black were taking off their fur coats. One of them he recognized as Ivan Ilyich's sister; the other was a stranger. Schwartz, his colleague, was just starting down the stairs, but on seeing Pyotr Ivanovich enter, he paused at the top step and winked at him as if to say: "Ivan Ilyich has really bungled—not the sort of thing you and I would do."

There was, as usual, an air of elegant solemnity about Schwartz, with his English sidewhiskers and his lean figure in a dress coat, and this solemnity, always such a marked contrast to his playful personality, had a special piquancy here. So, at least, Pyotr Ivanovich thought.

Pyotr Ivanovich stepped aside to let the ladies pass and slowly followed them up the stairs. Schwartz did not proceed downward but remained on the landing. Pyotr Ivanovich understood why; obviously, he wanted to arrange where they should play whist that evening. The ladies went upstairs to the widow's quarters, while Schwartz, his lips compressed into a serious expression and his eyes gleaming playfully, jerked his brows to the right to indicate the room where the dead man lay.

Pyotr Ivanovich went in bewildered, as people invariably are, about what he was expected to do there. The one thing he knew was that on such occasions it never did any harm to cross oneself. He was not quite certain whether he ought also to bow and so he adopted a middle course: on entering the room he began to cross himself and make a slight movement resembling a bow. At the same time, to the extent that the motions of his hands and head permitted, he glanced about the room. Two young people, apparently nephews, one of them a gymnasium student, were crossing themselves as they left the room. An old woman was standing motionless. And a lady with peculiarly arched brows was whispering something to her. A church reader in a frock coat—a vigorous, resolute fellow—was reading something in a loud voice and in a tone that brooked no contradiction. The pantry boy, Gerasim, stepped lightly in front of Pyotr Ivanovich, sprinkling something about the floor. Seeing this, Pyotr Ivanovich immediately became aware of a faint odor of decomposition. On his last visit Pyotr Ivanovich had seen this peasant boy in Ivan Ilyich's study; he had acted as a sick nurse to the dying man and Ivan Ilyich had been particularly fond of him.

Pyotr Ivanovich went on crossing himself and bowing slightly in a direction midway between the coffin, the church reader, and the icons on a table in the corner. Then, when he felt he had overdone the crossing, he paused and began to examine the dead man.

The body lay, as the dead invariably do, in a peculiarly heavy manner, with its rigid limbs sunk into the bedding of the coffin and its head eternally bowed on the pillow, exhibiting, as do all dead bodies, a yellow waxen forehead (with bald patches gleaming on the sunken temples), the protruding nose beneath seeming to press down against the upper lip. Ivan Ilyich had changed a great deal, grown even thinner since Pyotr Ivanovich had last seen him, and yet, as with all dead men, his face had acquired an expression of greater beauty—above all, of greater significance—than it had in life. Its expression implied that what needed to be done had been done and done properly. Moreover, there was in this expression a reproach or a reminder to the living. This reminder seemed out of place to Pyotr Ivanovich, or at least inapplicable to him. He began to feel somewhat uncomfortable and so he crossed himself hurriedly (all too hurriedly, he felt, from the standpoint of propriety), turned, and headed for the door.

In the adjoining room Schwartz was waiting for him, his feet planted solidly apart, his hands toying with the top hat he held behind his back. One glance at his playful, well-groomed, elegant figure was enough to revive Pyotr Ivanovich. He felt that Schwartz was above all this and would not succumb to mournful impressions. His very appearance seemed to say: "In no way can the incident of this funeral service for Ivan Ilyich be considered sufficient grounds for canceling the regular session; that is, nothing can prevent us from meeting tonight and flipping through a new deck of cards while a footman places four fresh candles around the table. There is, in fact, no reason to assume this incident can keep us from spending a pleasant evening." And he said as much to Pyotr Ivanovich in a whisper, proposing they meet for a game at Fyodor Vasilyevich's.

But Pyotr Ivanovich was not destined to play cards that evening. Praskovya Fyodorovna, a short, stocky woman (far broader at the hips than at the shoulders, despite all her efforts to the contrary), dressed all in black, with a lace shawl on her head and with the same peculiarly arched brows as the woman facing the coffin, emerged from her chambers with some other ladies whom she showed to the door of the room where the dead man lay, and said:

"The service is about to begin, do go in."

Schwartz made a vague sort of bow, then stopped, neither accepting nor rejecting the invitation. Recognizing Pyotr Ivanovich, Praskovya Fyodorovna sighed, went right up to him, took his hand, and said: "I know you were a true friend of Ivan Ilyich's . . ." and looked at him, awaiting a fitting response. Pyotr Ivanovich knew that just as he had to cross himself in there, here he had to press her hand, sigh, and say: "I assure you!" And so he did. And having done so felt he had achieved the desired effect: he was touched and so was she.

"Come, before it begins, I must have a talk with you," said the widow. "Give me your arm."

He gave her his arm and they proceeded toward the inner rooms, past Schwartz, who threw Pyotr Ivanovich a wink of regret that said: "So much for your card game. Don't be offended if we find another player. Perhaps you can make a fifth when you get away."

Pyotr Ivanovich sighed even more deeply and plaintively, and Praskovya Fyodorovna squeezed his hand gratefully. On entering her drawing room, decorated in pink cretonne and lit with a dim lamp, they sat down beside a table: she on a sofa, Pyotr Ivanovich on a low ottoman with broken springs that shifted under his weight. Praskovya Fyodorovna wanted to warn him against sitting there but felt such a warning was not in keeping with her situation and decided against it. As he sat down on the ottoman Pyotr Ivanovich recalled how, in decorating the room, Ivan Ilyich had consulted him about this pink cretonne with the green leaves. The whole room was crammed with furniture and knick-knacks, and as the widow stepped past the table to seat herself on the sofa, she entangled the lace of her black shawl in a bit of carving. Pyotr Ivanovich rose slightly to untangle it, and as he did the springs of the ottoman, freed of pressure, surged and gave him a little shove. The widow started to disentangle the lace herself and Pyotr Ivanovich sat down again, suppressing the rebellious springs beneath him. But the widow had not fully disentangled herself and Pyotr Ivanovich rose once again, and again the ottoman rebelled and even creaked. When all this was over, the widow took out a clean cambric handkerchief and began to weep. The episode with the lace and the battle with the ottoman had chilled Pyotr Ivanovich's emotions and he sat there scowling. The strain of the situation was broken when Sokolov, Ivan Ilyich's footman, came to report that the plot Praskovya Fyodorovna had selected in the cemetery would cost two hundred rubles. She stopped weeping and, glancing at Pyotr Ivanovich with a victimized air, told him in French how hard this was for her. He responded with a silent gesture indicating he had no doubt this was so.

"Please feel free to smoke," she said in a magnanimous yet crushed tone of voice and turned to Sokolov to discuss the price of the grave. As he lit his cigarette Pyotr Ivanovich heard her make detailed inquiries about the prices of various plots and arrive at a very sound decision. Moreover, when she had settled that matter, she made arrangements about the choristers. Then Sokolov left.

"I attend to everything myself," she said to Pyotr Ivanovich, moving aside some albums on the table. And noticing that the ashes of his cigarette were in danger of falling on the table, she quickly passed him an ashtray and said: "I believe it would be sheer pretense for me to say that I am unable, because of grief, to attend to practical matters. On the contrary, if anything can . . . I won't say console but . . . distract me, it is seeing to all these things about him." Again she took out a handkerchief as if about to weep but suddenly seemed to have mastered her emotion, and with a little toss of her head she began to speak calmly.

"But there is a matter I wish to discuss with you."

Pyotr Ivanovich bowed his head in response, taking care not to allow the springs of the ottoman, which immediately grew restive, to have their way.

"He suffered terribly the last few days."

"Did he?" asked Pyotr Ivanovich.

"Oh, frightfully! He screamed incessantly, not for minutes but for hours on end. He screamed for three straight days without pausing for breath. It was unbearable. I don't know how I bore up through it all. You could hear him three rooms away. Oh, what I've been through!"

"And was he really conscious through it all?" asked Pyotr Ivanovich.

"Yes," she whispered, "to the very last. He took leave of us a quarter of an hour before he died and even asked us to take Volodya away."

Despite a distasteful awareness of his own hypocrisy as well as hers, Pyotr Ivanovich was overcome with horror as he thought of the suffering of someone he had known so well, first as a carefree boy, then as a schoolmate, later as a grown man, his colleague. Once again he saw that forehead, that nose pressing down on the upper lip, and fear for himself took possession of him.

"Three days of terrible suffering and death. Why, the same thing could happen to me at anytime now," he thought and for a moment felt panic-stricken. But at once, he himself did not know how, he was rescued by the customary reflection that all this had happened to Ivan Ilyich, not to him, that it could not and should not happen to him; and that if he were to grant such a possibility, he would succumb to depression which, as Schwartz's expression had made abundantly clear, he ought not to do. With this line of reasoning Pyotr Ivanovich set his mind at rest and began to press for details about Ivan Ilyich's death, as though death were a chance experience that could happen only to Ivan Ilyich, never to himself.

After giving him various details about the truly horrible physical suffering Ivan Ilyich had endured (details which Pyotr Ivanovich learned strictly in terms of their unnerving effect upon

Praskovya Fyodorovna), the widow evidently felt it necessary to get down to business.

"Ah, Pyotr Ivanovich, how hard it is, how terribly, terribly hard," she said and again began weeping.

Pyotr Ivanovich sighed and waited for her to blow her nose. When she had, he said: "I assure you!..." and again she began to talk freely and got down to what was obviously her chief business with him: to ask how, in connection with her husband's death, she could obtain a grant of money from the government. She made it appear that she was asking Pyotr Ivanovich's advice about a pension, but he saw that she already knew more about this than he did, knew exactly, down to the finest detail, how much could be had from the government, but wanted to know if there was any possibility of extracting a bit more. Pyotr Ivanovich tried to think of some means of doing so, but after giving the matter a little thought and, for the sake of propriety, condemning the government for its stinginess, said he thought no more could be had. Whereupon she sighed and evidently tried to find some pretext for getting rid of her visitor. He surmised as much, put out his cigarette, stood up, shook her hand, and went out into the hall.

In the dining room with the clock which Ivan Ilyich had been so happy to have purchased at an antique shop, Pyotr Ivanovich met a priest and a few acquaintances who had come for the service, and he caught sight of a handsome young woman, Ivan Ilyich's daughter. She was dressed all in black, which made her slender waist appear even more so. She had a gloomy, determined, almost angry expression and bowed to Pyotr Ivanovich as if he were to blame for something. Behind her, with the same offended look, stood a rich young man Pyotr Ivanovich knew—an examining magistrate who, he had heard, was her fiancé. Pyotr Ivanovich gave them a mournful bow and was about to enter the dead man's room when Ivan Ilyich's son, a schoolboy who had an uncanny resemblance to his father, appeared from behind the stairwell. He was a small replica of the Ivan Ilyich whom Pyotr Ivanovich remembered from law school. His eyes were red from crying and had the look common to boys of thirteen or fourteen whose thoughts are no longer innocent. Seeing Pyotr Ivanovich, he frowned in a shamefaced way. Pyotr Ivanovich nodded to him and entered the room where the body lay. The service began: candles, groans, incense, tears, sobs. Pyotr Ivanovich stood with his brows knitted, staring at the feet of people in front of him. Never once did he look at the dead man or succumb to depression, and he was one of the first to leave. There was no one in the hallway, but Gerasim, the pantry boy, darted out of the dead man's room, rummaged with his strong hands through the mound of fur coats to find Pyotr Ivanovich's and helped him on with it.

"Well, Gerasim, my boy," said Pyotr Ivanovich in order to say something. "It's sad, isn't it?"

"It's God's will, sir. We all have to die someday," said Gerasim, displaying an even row of healthy white peasant teeth. And then, like a man in the thick of work, he briskly opened the door, shouted to the coachman, seated Pyotr Ivanovich in the carriage, and sprang back up the porch steps as though wondering what to do next.

After the smell of incense, the corpse, and the carbolic acid, Pyotr Ivanovich found it particularly pleasant to breathe in the fresh air.

"Where to, sir?" asked the coachman.

"It's not that late, I'll drop in at Fyodor Vasilyevich's."

And so he went. And when he arrived, he found they were just finishing the first rubber, so that it was convenient for him to make a fifth for the next.

Chapter 2

Ivan Ilyich's life had been most simple and commonplace—and most horrifying.

He died at the age of forty-five, a member of the Court of Justice. He was the son of an official who, in various Petersburg ministries and departments, had established the sort of career whereby men reach a stage at which, owing to their rank and years of service, they cannot be dismissed, even though they are clearly unfit for any responsible work; and therefore they receive fictitious appointments, especially designed for them, and by no means fictitious salaries of from six to ten thousand on which they live to a ripe old age.

Such was the Privy Councillor Ilya Efimovich Golovin, superfluous member of various superfluous institutions.

He had three sons, of whom Ivan Ilyich was the second. The eldest had established the same type of career as his father, except in a different ministry, and was rapidly approaching the stage where men obtain sinecures. The third son was a failure. He had ruined his prospects in a number of positions and was now serving in the Railway Division. His father and brothers, and especially their wives, not only hated meeting him but, unless compelled to do otherwise, managed to forget his existence. The sister had married

Baron Greff, the same sort of Petersburg official as his father-in-law. Ivan Ilyich, as they said, was *le phénix de la famille*. He was neither as cold and punctilious as his elder brother nor as reckless as his younger. He was a happy mean between the two—a clever, lively, pleasant, and respectable man. He and his younger brother had both attended the school of jurisprudence. The younger brother never graduated, for he was expelled when he reached the fifth course. On the other hand, Ivan Ilyich completed the program creditably. As a law student he had become exactly what he was to remain the rest of his life: a capable, cheerful, good-natured, and sociable man but one strict to carry out whatever he considered his duty, and he considered his duty all things that were so designated by people in authority. Neither as a boy nor as an adult had he been a toady, but from his earliest youth he had been drawn to people of high standing in society as a moth is to light; he had adopted their manners and their views on life and had established friendly relations with them. All the enthusiasms of childhood and youth passed, leaving no appreciable impact on him; he had succumbed to sensuality and vanity and, in his last years at school, to liberalism, but strictly within the limits his instinct unerringly prescribed.

As a student he had done things which, at the time, seemed to him extremely vile and made him feel disgusted with himself; but later, seeing that people of high standing had no qualms about doing these things, he was not quite able to consider them good but managed to dismiss them and not feel the least perturbed when he recalled them.

When he graduated from law school with a degree qualifying him for the tenth rank of the civil service, and had obtained money from his father for his outfit, he ordered some suits at Sharmer's, the fashionable tailor, hung a medallion inscribed *respice finem* on his watch chain, took leave of his mentor and prince, who was patron of the school, dined in state with his friends at Donon's, and then, with fashionable new luggage, linen, clothes, shaving and other toilet articles, and a traveling rug (all ordered and purchased at the finest shops), he set off for one of the provinces to assume a post his father had secured for him there as assistant on special commissions to the governor.

Ivan Ilyich immediately made his life in the provinces as easy and pleasant as it had been at law school. He worked, saw to his career, and, at the same time, engaged in proper and pleasant forms of diversion. When from time to time he traveled to country districts on official business, he maintained his dignity with both his superiors and inferiors and fulfilled the duties entrusted to him (primarily cases involving a group of religious sectarians) with an exactitude and incorruptibility in which he could only take pride.

In his official duties, despite his youth and love of light forms of amusement, he was exceedingly reserved, punctilious, and even severe; but in society he was often playful and witty, always good-humored and polite—a *bon enfant*, as the governor and his wife, with whom he was like one of the family, used to say of him.

In the provinces he had an affair with one of the ladies who threw themselves at the chic young lawyer; there was also a milliner: there were drinking bouts with visiting aides-de-camp and after-supper trips to a certain street on the outskirts of town; there were also attempts to curry favor with his chief and even with his chief's wife. But all this had such a heightened air of respectability that nothing bad could be said about it. It could all be summed up by the French saying: *"Il faut que jeunesse se passe."* It was all done with clean hands, in clean shirts, and with French phrases, and, most importantly, among people of the best society—consequently, with the approval of those in high rank.

Ivan Ilyich spent five years of his service career in this manner, and at the end of that time there was a change in his official life. New judicial institutions had been formed and new men were needed.

Ivan Ilyich became such a new man.

He was offered a post as examining magistrate and he accepted it, even though it meant moving to another province, giving up the connections he had formed, and establishing new ones. His friends met to bid him farewell: they had a group photograph taken and presented him with a silver cigarette case, and he set off to assume his new position.

As an examining magistrate, Ivan Ilyich was just as *comme il faut* and respectable, just as capable of separating his official duties from his private life and of inspiring general respect as he had been while acting as assistant on special commissions. He found the work of a magistrate far more interesting and appealing than his former duties. In his previous position he had enjoyed the opportunity to stride freely and easily in his Sharmer uniform past the crowd of anxious, envious petitioners and officials waiting to be heard by the governor, to go straight into his chief's office and sit with him over a cup of tea and a cigarette. But few people had been directly under his control then—only the district police officers and religious sectarians he encountered when sent out on special commissions. And he loved to treat these people courteously, almost as comrades, loved to make them feel that he who had the power to crush them was dealing with them in such a friendly, unpretentious manner. But there had been few such people. Now, as an examining magistrate, Ivan Ilyich felt that all, without exception—including the most important and self-satisfied people—all were in his power, and that he had only to write certain words on a sheet of paper with an official heading and this or that important, self-satisfied person would be brought to him as a defendant or a witness, and if Ivan Ilyich did not choose to have him sit, he would be forced to stand and answer his questions. Ivan Ilyich never abused his power; on the contrary, he tried to exercise it leniently; but the awareness of that power and the opportunity to be lenient constituted the chief interest and appeal of his new post. In the work itself—that is, in conducting investigations—Ivan Ilyich soon mastered the technique of dispensing with all considerations that did not pertain to his job as examining magistrate, and of writing up even the most complicated cases in a style that reduced them to their externals, bore no trace of his personal opinion, and, most importantly, adhered to all the prescribed formalities. This type of work was new, and he was one of the first men to give practical application to the judicial reforms instituted by the Code of 1864.

On taking up the post of examining magistrate in the new town, Ivan Ilyich made new acquaintances and connections, adopted a new stance, and assumed a somewhat different tone. He put a suitable amount of distance between himself and the provincial authorities, chose his friends from among the best circle of lawyers and wealthy gentry in the town, and assumed an air of mild dissatisfaction with the government, of moderate liberalism, of enlightened civic responsibility. And though he remained as fastidious as ever about his attire, he stopped shaving his chin and allowed his beard to grow freely.

In the new town, too, life turned out to be very pleasant for Ivan Ilyich. The people opposed to the governor were friendly and congenial, his salary was higher, and he began to play whist, which added considerably to the pleasure of his life, for he had an ability to maintain his good spirits while playing and to reason quickly and subtly, so that he usually came out ahead.

After he had been working in the town for two years, Ivan Ilyich met his future wife. Praskovya Fyodorovna Mikhel was the most attractive, intelligent, and outstanding young lady of the set in which Ivan Ilyich moved. In addition to the other amusements and relaxations that provided relief from his work as an examining magistrate, Ivan Ilyich began a light flirtation with Praskovya Fyodorovna.

As an assistant on special commissions Ivan Ilyich had, as a rule, danced; as an examining magistrate he danced as an exception. He danced to show that although he was a representative of the reformed legal institutions and an official of the fifth rank, when it came to dancing, he could also excel at that. So he occasionally danced with Praskovya Fyodorovna at the end of an evening, and it was mainly during the time they danced together that he conquered her. She fell in love with him. Ivan Ilyich had no clear and definite intention of marrying, but when the girl fell in love with him, he asked himself: "Really, why shouldn't I get married?"

Praskovya Fyodorovna came from a good family and was quite attractive; she also had a little money. Ivan Ilyich could have counted on a more illustrious match, but even this one was quite good. He had his salary, and her income, he hoped, would bring in an equal amount. It would be a good alliance: she was a sweet, pretty, and extremely well-bred young woman. To say that Ivan Ilyich married because he fell in love with his fiancée and found her sympathetic to his views on life would be as mistaken as to say that he married because the people in his circle approved of the match. Ivan Ilyich married for both reasons: in acquiring such a wife he did something that gave him pleasure and, at the same time, did what people of the highest standing considered correct.

And so Ivan Ilyich got married.

The preparations for marriage and the first period of married life, with its conjugal caresses, new furniture, new dishes, new linen—the period up to his wife's pregnancy—went very well, so that Ivan Ilyich began to think that marriage would not disrupt the easy, pleasant, cheerful, and respectable life approved of by society (a pattern he believed to be universal); that it would even enhance such a life. But during the first months of his wife's pregnancy, something new, unexpected, and disagreeable manifested itself, something painful and unseemly, which he had no way of anticipating and could do nothing to avoid.

For no reason at all, so it seemed to Ivan Ilyich—*de gaîté de cœur*, as he told himself—his wife began to undermine the pleasure and propriety of their life: she became jealous without cause, demanded he be more attentive to her, found fault with everything, and created distasteful and ill-mannered scenes.

At first Ivan Ilyich hoped to escape from this unpleasant state of affairs by preserving the same carefree and proper approach to life that had served him in the past. He tried to ignore his wife's bad moods, went on living in a pleasant and easygoing fashion, invited friends over for cards, and made an effort to get away to his club or his friends' homes. But on one occasion his wife lashed out at him with such fury and such foul language, and persisted in attacking him every time he failed to satisfy her demands (apparently having resolved not to let up until he submitted—that is, until he stayed home and moped as she did) that Ivan Ilyich was horrified. He realized that married life—at least with his wife—was not always conducive to the pleasures and proprieties of life but, on the contrary, frequently disrupted them, and for that reason he must guard against such disruptions. Ivan Ilyich tried to find some means of doing this. His work was the one thing that made any impression on Praskovya Fyodorovna, and so he began to use his work and the obligations it entailed as a way of combating his wife and safeguarding his independence.

With the birth of the baby, the attempts to feed it and the various difficulties, the real and imaginary illnesses of mother and child, which Ivan Ilyich was supposed to sympathize with but failed to understand, his need to fence off a world for himself outside the family became even more imperative.

To the degree that his wife became more irritable and demanding, Ivan Ilyich increasingly made work the center of gravity in his life. He grew more attached to his job and more ambitious than before.

Very soon, within a year after his wedding, Ivan Ilyich realized that married life, though it offered certain conveniences, was in fact a very complex and difficult business, and that to do one's duty to it—that is, to lead a proper, socially acceptable life—one had to develop a clearly defined attitude to it, just as one did with respect to work.

And Ivan Ilyich developed such an attitude. Of married life he demanded only the conveniences it could provide—dinners at home, a well-run household, a partner in bed, and, above all, a veneer of respectability which public opinion required. As for the rest, he tried to find enjoyment in family life, and, if he succeeded, was very grateful; but if he met with resistance and querulousness, he immediately withdrew into his separate, entrenched world of work and found pleasure there.

Ivan Ilyich was esteemed for his diligent service, and after three years he was made assistant public prosecutor. His new duties, the importance of them, the possibility of indicting and imprisoning anyone he chose, the publicity his speeches received and the success they brought him—all this further enhanced the appeal of his work.

Other children were born. His wife became more and more petulant and irascible, but the attitude Ivan Ilyich had adopted toward domestic life made him almost impervious to her carping.

After serving for seven years in this town, Ivan Ilyich was transferred to another province as public prosecutor. They moved, they were short of money, and his wife disliked the new town. Although his salary was higher, the cost of living was greater; moreover, two of their children had died, and so family life became even more unpleasant for Ivan Ilyich.

Praskovya Fyodorovna blamed her husband for every setback they experienced in the new town. Most of the topics of conversation between husband and wife, especially the children's education, brought up issues on which they remembered having quarreled, and these quarrels were apt to flare up again at any moment. All they had left were the rare periods of amorousness that came over them, but these did not last long. They were merely little islands at which the couple anchored for a while before setting out again on a sea of veiled hostility, which took the form of estrangement from one another. This estrangement might have distressed Ivan Ilyich had he felt it should not exist, but by now he not only regarded it as a normal state of affairs, but as a goal he sought to achieve in family life. That goal was to free himself more and more from these disturbances, to make them appear innocuous and respectable. He managed to do this by spending less and less time with his family and, when obliged to be at home, tried to safeguard his position through the presence of outsiders. But what mattered most was that Ivan Ilyich had his work. His entire interest in life was centered in the world of official duties and that interest totally absorbed him. The awareness of his power, the chance to ruin whomever he chose, the importance attached even to his entry into the courtroom and manner of conferring with his subordinates, the success he enjoyed both with them and his superiors, and, above all, his own recognition of the skill with which he handled cases—all this gave him cause for rejoicing and, together with chats with his colleagues, dinner invitations, and whist, made his life full. So that on the whole Ivan Ilyich's life proceeded as he felt it should—pleasantly and properly.

He went on living this way for another seven years. His daughter was then sixteen years old, another child had died, and one son remained, a schoolboy, the subject of dissension. Ivan Il-yich wanted to send him to the school of juris-prudence, but out of spite Praskovya Fyodo-rovna enrolled him in the gymnasium. The daughter had studied at home and made good progress; the boy, too, was a rather good student.

Chapter 3

Ivan Ilyich spent seventeen years of his married life this way. He was already an experienced public prosecutor who had declined several positions in the hope of obtaining a more desirable one, when an unforeseen and unpleasant circumstance virtually disrupted the peaceful course of his life. He expected to be appointed presiding judge in a university town, but Hoppe managed to move in ahead and get the appointment. Ivan Ilyich was infuriated, made accusations, and quarreled with Hoppe and his immediate superiors. They began to treat him with disdain and during the next round of appointments again passed him by.

This happened in 1880, the most difficult year in Ivan Ilyich's life. For one thing, it turned out that he could not make ends meet on his salary; for another, that he had been neglected, and that what he considered the most outrageous, heartless injustice appeared to others as quite commonplace. Even his father did not consider it his duty to help him. Ivan Ilyich felt that everyone had abandoned him, convinced that the position of a man earning three thousand five hundred rubles was entirely normal and even fortunate. He alone knew that what with the injustices he had suffered, his wife's incessant nagging, and the debts he had incurred by living above his means, his position was far from normal.

That summer, in order to save money, he took a leave of absence and went to the country with his wife to live at her brother's place. In the country, with no work to do, Ivan Ilyich for the first time in his life experienced not only boredom but intolerable anguish; he decided that he simply could not go on living this way, that he had to take some decisive measures.

After a sleepless night spent pacing the terrace, he made up his mind to go to Petersburg and punish *those people*—those who had failed to appreciate him—by trying to get himself transferred to another ministry.

The next day, despite all the efforts of his wife and his brother-in-law to dissuade him, he set off for Petersburg. He had only one purpose in going: to obtain a post with a salary of five thousand rubles. He was no longer bent on any particular ministry, field, or type of work. He only wanted a post that would pay him five thousand; it could be a post with the administration, the banks, the railways, the Dowager Empress Maria's charitable institutions, or even the customs office, but it had to pay five thousand and allow him to stop working for a ministry that failed to appreciate him.

And his trip was crowned with amazing and unexpected success. At Kursk an acquaintance of his, F. S. Ilyin, boarded the train, sat down in the first-class carriage, and told Ivan Ilyich that the governor of Kursk had just received a telegram announcing an important change of staff that was about to take place in the ministry: Ivan Semyonovich was to replace Pyotr Ivanovich.

The proposed change, in addition to the significance it had for Russia, was of particular significance for Ivan Ilyich, since it brought to power a new man, Pyotr Petrovich, and, it appeared, his friend Zakhar Ivanovich—a circumstance that was highly favorable for Ivan Ilyich. Zakhar Ivanovich was a colleague and friend of his.

In Moscow the news was confirmed, and on reaching Petersburg, Ivan Ilyich looked up Zakhar Ivanovich, who guaranteed him an appointment in the Ministry of Justice where he had served before.

A week later he telegraphed his wife: "Zakhar in Miller's place. With first report I receive appointment."

Thanks to this change of staff, Ivan Ilyich unexpectedly received an appointment in his former ministry that placed him two ranks above his colleagues, paid him a salary of five thousand rubles, and provided an additional three thousand five hundred for the expenses of relocation. His resentment against his former enemies and the whole ministry vanished completely and he was perfectly happy.

Ivan Ilyich returned to the country more cheerful and contented than he had been in some time. Praskovya Fyodorovna's spirits also picked up, and they concluded a truce. Ivan Ilyich told her how he had been honored in Petersburg, how all his enemies had been disgraced and fawned on him now and envied his position; and he made a point of telling her how much everyone in Petersburg had liked him.

Praskovya Fyodorovna listened, pretended to believe all of this, never once contradicted him, and devoted herself exclusively to making plans for their life in the city to which they were moving. And Ivan Ilyich was delighted to see that her plans were his, that he and his wife were in agreement, and that after a little stumble his life was resuming its genuine and natural quality of carefree pleasure and propriety.

Ivan Ilyich had come back for only a brief stay. On the tenth of September he had to assume his new position; moreover, he needed time to get settled in the new place, to move all their belongings from the provinces, to buy and order a great many more things. In short, to arrange their life in the style he had set his mind to (which corresponded almost exactly to the style Praskovya Fyodorovna had set her heart on).

Now that everything had worked out so well and he and his wife were at one in their aims and, in addition, saw very little of each other, they were closer than they had been since the first years of their married life. Ivan Ilyich had intended to take his family with him at once, but at the urging of his sister-in-law and brother-in-law, who suddenly became unusually amiable and warm to Ivan Ilyich and his family, he set off alone.

He set off, and the happy frame of mind induced by his success and the understanding

with his wife, the one intensifying the other,
never once deserted him. He found a charming
apartment, exactly what he and his wife had
dreamed of. Spacious reception rooms with high
ceilings in the old style, a magnificent and comfortable study, rooms for his wife and daughter,
a study room for his son—all as though it had
been designed especially for them. Ivan Ilyich
himself undertook the decorating, selecting the
wallpaper and the upholstery, purchasing more
furniture, mostly antiques, which he thought
particularly *comme il faut*, and everything progressed until it began to approach the ideal he
had set himself. When only half the decorating
had been completed, the result exceeded his ex-
pectations. He sensed how elegant and refined
an atmosphere, free of vulgarity, the whole place
would acquire when it was finished. As he fell
asleep he pictured to himself how the reception
room would look. When he glanced at the un-
finished drawing room he conjured up an image
of the fireplace, the screen, the what-not, the
little chairs scattered here and there, the plates
and china on the walls, and the bronzes, as they
would appear when everything was in place. He
was thrilled to think how he would surprise
Pasha and Lizanka, who also had good taste in
these matters. They had no idea what was in
store for them. He had been particularly successful at finding and making inexpensive pur-
chases of old furniture, which added a decidedly
aristocratic tone to the whole place. In his letters
to his family he deliberately understated everything in order to surprise them. All this was so

engrossing that even his new post, work he loved, absorbed him less than he had expected. During court sessions he sometimes became distracted, wondering whether he should have straight or curved cornices for the draperies. He was so preoccupied with these matters that he often did some of the work himself—rearranged the furniture, rehung the draperies. Once, when he mounted a stepladder to show a perplexed upholsterer how he wanted the draperies hung, he missed a step and fell, but being a strong and agile man, he held on to the ladder and merely banged his side against the knob of the window frame. The bruise hurt for a while, but the pain soon disappeared. All through this period Ivan Ilyich felt particularly well and cheerful. "I feel fifteen years younger," he wrote his family. He expected to finish in September, but the work dragged on until mid-October. Yet the result was stunning—an opinion voiced not only by him but by everyone else who saw the place.

In actuality, it was like the homes of all people who are not really rich but who want to look rich, and therefore end up looking like one another: it had damasks, ebony, plants, carpets, and bronzes, everything dark and gleaming—all the effects a certain class of people produce so as to look like people of a certain class. And his place looked so much like the others that it would never have been noticed, though it all seemed quite exceptional to him. When he met his family at the station and brought them back to their brightly lit furnished apartment, and a footman in a white tie opened the door to a flower-be-decked entrance hall, from which they proceeded to the drawing room and the study, gasping with delight, he was very happy, showed them everywhere, drank in their praises and beamed with satisfaction. At tea that evening when, among other things, Praskovya Fyodorovna asked him about his fall, he laughed and gave them a comic demonstration of how he had gone flying off the stepladder and frightened the upholsterer.

"It's a good thing I'm so agile. Another man would have killed himself, but I got off with just a little bump here; it hurts when I touch it, but it's already beginning to clear up—it's just a bruise."

And so they began to live in their new quarters which, as always happens when people get settled, was just one room too small, and on their new income which, as is always the case, was just a bit less—about five hundred rubles—than they needed. But it was all very nice. It was particularly nice in the beginning, before the apartment was fully arranged and some work still had to be done: this thing bought, that thing ordered, another thing moved, still another adjusted. And while there were some disagreements between husband and wife, both were so pleased and had so much to do that it all passed off without any major quarrels. When there was no work left to be done, it became a bit dull and something seemed to be lacking, but by then they were making acquaintances, forming new habits, and life was full.

Ivan Ilyich spent his mornings in court and

came home for dinner, and at first he was in fine spirits, though it was precisely the apartment that caused him some distress. (Every spot on the tablecloth or the upholstery, every loose cord on the draperies irritated him; he had gone to such pains with the decorating that any damage to it upset him.) But on the whole Ivan Ilyich's life moved along as he believed life should: easily, pleasantly, and properly. He got up at nine, had his coffee, read the newspapers, then put on his uniform and went to court. There the harness in which he worked had already been worn into shape and he slipped right into it: petitioners, inquiries sent to the office, the office itself, the court sessions—preliminary and public. In all this one had to know how to exclude whatever was fresh and vital, which always disrupted the course of official business: one could have only official relations with people, and only on official grounds, and the relations themselves had to be kept purely official. For instance, a man would come and request some information. As an official who was charged with other duties, Ivan Ilyich could not have any dealings with such a man; but if the man approached him about a matter that related to his function as a court member, then within the limits of this relationship Ivan Ilyich would do everything, absolutely everything he could for him and, at the same time, maintain a semblance of friendly, human relations—that is, treat him with civility. As soon as the official relations ended, so did all the rest. Ivan Ilyich had a superb ability to detach the official aspect of things from his real life, and thanks to his talent and years of experience, he had cultivated it to such a degree that occasionally, like a virtuoso, he allowed himself to mix human and official relations, as if for fun. He allowed himself this liberty because he felt he had the strength to isolate the purely official part of the relationship again, if need be, and discard the human. And he did so not only in an easy, pleasant, and proper manner, but with style. In between times he smoked, had tea, talked a little about politics, a little about general matters, but most of all about appointments. And then tired, but with the feeling of a virtuoso—one of the first violinists in an orchestra who had played his part superbly—he would return home. There he would find that his wife and daughter had been out paying calls or had a visitor; that his son had been to the gymnasium, had gone over his lessons with a tutor, and was diligently learning all that students are taught in the gymnasium. Everything was just fine. After dinner, if there were no guests, Ivan Ilyich sometimes read a book that was the talk of the day and in the evening settled down to work—that is, read official papers, checked laws, compared depositions, and classified them according to the legal statutes. He found such work neither boring nor engaging. It was a bore if it meant foregoing a card game, but if there was no game on, it was better than sitting home alone or with his wife. Ivan Ilyich derived pleasure from giving small dinner parties to which he invited men and women of good social standing; and the dinners he gave resembled the ones they usually gave as much as his drawing room looked like all the other drawing rooms.

Once they even had an evening party with dancing. Ivan Ilyich was in fine spirits and everything went off well except that he had an enormous fight with his wife over the pastries and bonbons. Praskovya Fyodorovna had her own plans about these, but Ivan Ilyich insisted on ordering everything from an expensive confectioner; he ordered a great many pastries, and the quarrel broke out because some of the pastries were left over and the bill came to forty-five rubles. It was such an enormous, nasty fight that Praskovya Fyodorovna called him an "imbecile" and a "spoiler," while he clutched his head and inwardly muttered something about a divorce. But the party itself was gay. The best people came and Ivan Ilyich danced with Princess Trufonova, sister of the Trufonova who had founded the charitable society called "Take My Grief Upon Thee."

The pleasures Ivan Ilyich derived from his work were those of pride; the pleasures he derived from society those of vanity; but it was genuine pleasure that he derived from playing whist. He confessed that no matter what happened, regardless of all the unhappiness he might experience, there was one pleasure which, like a bright candle, outshone all the others in his life: that was to sit down with some good players, quiet partners, to a game of whist, definitely a four-handed game (with five players it was painful to sit out, even though one pretended not to mind), to play a clever, serious game (when the cards permitted), then have supper and drink a glass of wine. After a game of whist, especially if he had won a little (winning a lot was distasteful), Ivan Ilyich went to bed in a particularly good mood.

So they lived. They moved in the best circles and their home was frequented by people of importance and by the young. There was complete accord between husband, wife, and daughter about their set of acquaintances and, without discussing the matter, they were equally adept at brushing off and escaping from various shabby friends and relations who, with a great show of affection, descended on them in their drawing room with the Japanese plates on the walls. Soon these shabby friends stopped intruding and the Golovins' set included only the best. Young men courted Lizanka, and the examining magistrate Petrishchev, the son and sole heir of Dmitry Ivanovich Petrishchev, was so attentive that Ivan Ilyich talked to Praskovya Fyodorovna about having a sleighing party for them or arranging some private theatricals.

So they lived. Everything went along without change and everything was fine.

Chapter 4

They were all in good health. Ivan Ilyich
sometimes complained of a strange taste in his
mouth and some discomfort in his left side, but
this could hardly be called ill health.

Yet the discomfort increased, and although
it had not developed into real pain, the sense of
a constant pressure in his side made Ivan Ilyich
ill-tempered. His irritability became progres-
sively more marked and began to spoil the pleasure of the easy and proper life that had only
recently been established in the Golovin family.
Husband and wife began to quarrel more often,
and soon the ease and pleasure disappeared and
even the propriety was barely maintained. Scenes
became more frequent. Once again there were
only little islands, very few at that, on which
husband and wife could meet without an explo-
sion.

Praskovya Fyodorovna had good reason
now for saying that her husband had a trying
disposition. With her characteristic tendency to
exaggerate, she said he had always had such a
horrid disposition and that only someone with
her goodness of heart could have put up with it
for twenty years. It was true that he was the one
now who started the arguments. He invariably
began cavilling when he sat down to dinner—
often just as he was starting on his soup. Either

he noticed that a dish was chipped, or the food was not good, or his son had put his elbow on the table, or his daughter had not combed her hair properly. And for all this he blamed Praskovya Fyodorovna. At first she fought back and said nasty things to him, but once or twice at the start of dinner he flew into such a rage that she realized it was due to some physical discomfort provoked by eating, and so she restrained herself and did not answer back but merely tried to get dinner over with as quickly as possible. Praskovya Fyodorovna regarded her self-restraint as a great virtue. Having concluded that her husband had a horrid disposition and had made her life miserable, she began to pity herself. And the more she pitied herself, the more she hated her husband. She began to wish he would die, yet she could not really wish that, for then there would be no income. This made her even more incensed with him. She considered herself supremely unhappy because even his death could not save her. She was exasperated yet concealed it, and her suppressed exasperation only heightened his exasperation.

After a scene in which Ivan Ilyich had been particularly unjust and, by way of explanation, admitted being irritable but attributed this to illness, she told him that if he was ill he must be treated, and she insisted he go and consult a celebrated physician.

He did. The whole procedure was just what he expected, just what one always encounters. There was the waiting, the doctor's exaggerated air of importance (so familiar to him since it was the very air he assumed in court), the tapping, the listening, the questions requiring answers that were clearly superfluous since they were foregone conclusions, and the significant look that implied: "Just put yourself in our hands and we'll take care of everything; we know exactly what has to be done—we always use one and the same method for every patient, no matter who." Everything was just as it was in court. The celebrated doctor dealt with him in precisely the manner he dealt with men on trial.

The doctor said: such and such indicates that you have such and such, but if an analysis of such and such does not confirm this, then we have to assume you have such and such. On the other hand, if we assume such and such is the case, then . . . and so on. To Ivan Ilyich only one question mattered: was his condition serious or not? But the doctor ignored this inappropriate question. From his point of view it was an idle question and not worth considering. One simply had to weigh the alternatives: a floating kidney, chronic catarrh, or a disease of the caecum. It was not a matter of Ivan Ilyich's life but a conflict between a floating kidney and a disease of the caecum. And in Ivan Ilyich's presence the doctor resolved that conflict brilliantly in favor of the caecum, with the reservation that if an analysis of the urine yielded new evidence, the case would be reconsidered. This was exactly what Ivan Ilyich had done a thousand times, and in the same brilliant manner, with prisoners in the dock. The doctor summed up just as brilliantly, glancing triumphantly, even jovially, over his glasses at the prisoner. From the doctor's summary Ivan Ilyich concluded that things were bad, but that to the doctor and perhaps everyone else, it was of no consequence, even though for him it was bad. And this conclusion, which came as a painful shock to Ivan Ilyich, aroused in him a feeling of great self-pity and equally great resentment toward the doctor for being so indifferent to a matter of such importance.

But he made no comment, he simply got up, put his fee on the table, heaved a sigh, and said: "No doubt we sick people often ask inappropriate questions. But, in general, would you say my illness is serious or not?"

The doctor cocked one eye sternly at him over his glasses as if to say: "Prisoner, if you do not confine yourself to the questions allowed, I shall be obliged to have you expelled from the courtroom."

"I have already told you what I consider necessary and suitable," said the doctor. "Anything further will be revealed by the analysis." And with a bow the doctor brought the visit to a close.

Ivan Ilyich went out slowly, seated himself despondently in his sledge and drove home. All the way home he kept going over in his mind what the doctor had said, trying to translate all those vague, confusing scientific terms into simple language and find an answer to his question: "Is my condition serious? Very serious? Or nothing much to worry about?" And it seemed to him that the essence of what the doctor had said was that it was very serious. Everything in the streets seemed dismal to Ivan Ilyich. The cab drivers looked dismal, the houses looked dismal, the passersby, the shops—everything looked dismal. And in light of the doctor's obscure remarks, that pain—that dull, nagging pain which never let up for a second—acquired a different, a more serious implication. Ivan Ilyich focused on it now with a new sense of distress.

He reached home and began telling his wife about the visit. She listened, but in the middle of his account his daughter came in with her hat on—she and her mother were preparing to go out. She forced herself to sit and listen to this tedious stuff but could not stand it for long, and his wife, too, did not hear him out.

"Well, I'm very glad," she said. "Now see to it you take your medicine regularly. Give me the prescription, I'll send Gerasim to the apothecary's." And she went off to dress.

While she was in the room Ivan Ilyich had scarcely paused for breath, but he heaved a deep sigh when she left.

"Well," he said, "maybe there's nothing much to worry about."

He began to take the medicine and follow the doctor's instructions, which were changed after the analysis of his urine. But then it appeared that there was some confusion between the results of the analysis and what should have followed from it. It was impossible to get any information out of the doctor, but somehow things were not working out as he had said they should. Either the doctor had overlooked something, or lied, or concealed something from him.

Nonetheless, Ivan Ilyich followed his instructions explicitly and at first derived some comfort from this.

After his visit to the doctor, Ivan Ilyich was preoccupied mainly with attempts to carry out the doctor's orders about hygiene, medicine, observation of the course of his pain, and all his bodily functions. His main interests in life became human ailments and human health. Whenever there was any talk in his presence of people who were sick, or who had died or recuperated, particularly from an illness resembling his own, he would listen intently, trying to conceal his agitation, ask questions, and apply what he learned to his own case.

The pain did not subside, but Ivan Ilyich forced himself to think he was getting better. And he managed to deceive himself as long as nothing upset him. But no sooner did he have a nasty episode with his wife, a setback at work, or a bad hand at cards, than he immediately became acutely aware of his illness. In the past he had been able to cope with such adversities, confident that in no time at all he would set things right, get the upper hand, succeed, have a grand slam. Now every setback knocked the ground out from under him and reduced him to despair. He would say to himself: "There, just as I was beginning to get better and the medicine was taking effect, this accursed misfortune or trouble had to happen." And he raged against misfortune or against the people who were causing him trouble and killing him, for he felt his rage was killing him but could do nothing to control it. One would have expected him to understand that the anger he vented on people and circumstances only aggravated his illness and that, consequently, the thing to do was to disregard unpleasant occurrences. But his reasoning took just the opposite turn: he said he needed peace, was on the lookout for anything that might disturb it, and at the slightest disturbance became exasperated. What made matters worse was that he read medical books and consulted doctors. His condition deteriorated so gradually that he could easily deceive himself when comparing one day with the next—the difference was that slight. But when he consulted doctors, he felt he was not only deteriorating but at a very rapid rate. And in spite of this he kept on consulting them.

That month he went to see another celebrated physician. This celebrity told him practically the same thing as the first but posed the problem somewhat differently. And the consultation with this celebrity only reinforced Ivan Ilyich's doubts and fears. A friend of a friend—a very fine doctor—diagnosed the case quite differently, and though he assured Ivan Ilyich that he would recover, his questions and suppositions only made him more confused and heightened his suspicions. A homeopath offered still another diagnosis and prescribed certain medicine, and for about a week Ivan Ilyich took it without telling anyone. But when a week passed with no sign of relief, he lost faith in both this and the previous types of treatment and became even more despondent.

Once a lady he knew told him about a cure effected with wonder-working icons. Ivan Ilyich caught himself listening intently and believing in the possibility. This incident alarmed him. "Have I really become so gullible?" he asked himself. "Nonsense! It's all rubbish. Instead of giving in to these nervous fears, I've got to choose one doctor and stick to his method of treatment. That's just what I'll do. Enough! I'll stop thinking about it and follow the doctor's orders strictly until summer and then see what happens. No more wavering!"

It was an easy thing to say but impossible to do. The pain in his side exhausted him, never let up, seemed to get worse all the time; the taste in his mouth became more and more peculiar; he felt his breath had a foul odor; his appetite diminished and he kept losing strength. There was no deceiving himself: something new and dreadful was happening to him, something of such vast importance that nothing in his life could compare with it. And he alone was aware of this. Those about him either did not understand or did not wish to understand and thought that nothing in the world had changed. It was precisely this which tormented Ivan Ilyich most of all. He saw that the people in his household—particularly his wife and daughter, who were caught up in a whirl of social activity—had no understanding of what was happening and were vexed with him for being so disconsolate and demanding, as though he were to blame. Although they tried to conceal this, he saw that he was an obstacle to them, and that his wife had adopted a certain attitude toward his illness and clung to it regardless of what he said or did. Her attitude amounted to this: "You know," she would say to her acquaintances, "Ivan Ilyich, like most people, simply cannot adhere to the course of treatment prescribed for him. One day he takes his drops, sticks to his diet, and goes to bed on time. But if I don't keep an eye on him, the next day he'll forget to take his medicine, eat sturgeon—which is forbidden—and sit up until one o'clock in the morning playing cards."

"Oh, when was that?" Ivan Ilyich retorted peevishly. "Only once at Pyotr Ivanovich's."

"And last night with Shebek."

"What difference did it make? I couldn't sleep anyway because of the pain."

"Well, it really doesn't matter why you did it, but if you go on like this, you'll never get well and just keep on torturing us."

From the remarks she made to both him and others, Praskovya Fyodorovna's attitude toward her husband's illness was that he himself was to blame for it, and that the whole thing was simply another way of making her life unpleasant. Ivan Ilyich felt that these remarks escaped her involuntarily, but this did not make things any easier for him.

In court, too, Ivan Ilyich noticed, or thought he noticed, a strange attitude toward himself. At times he felt people were eyeing him closely as a man whose post would soon be vacant; at other times his friends suddenly began teasing him, in a friendly way, about his nervous fears, as though that horrid, appalling, unheard-of something that had been set in motion within him and was gnawing away at him day and night, ineluctably dragging him off somewhere, was a most agreeable subject for a joke. He was particularly irritated by Schwartz, whose playfulness, vivacity, and *comme il faut* manner reminded him of himself ten years earlier.

Friends came over to make up a set and sat down to a game of cards with him. They dealt, bending the new cards to soften them; Ivan Ilyich sorted the diamonds in his hand and found he had seven. His partner said: "No trumps," and supported him with two diamonds. What more could he have wished for? He ought to have felt cheered, invigorated—they would make a grand slam. But suddenly Ivan Ilyich became aware of that gnawing pain in his side, that taste in his mouth, and under the circumstances it seemed preposterous to him to rejoice in a grand slam.

He saw his partner, Mikhail Mikhailovich, rapping the table with a vigorous hand, courteously and indulgently refraining from snatching up the tricks, pushing them over to him, so that he could have the pleasure of picking them up without having to exert himself. "Does he think I'm so weak I can't stretch my hand out?" Ivan Ilyich thought, and forgetting what he was doing, he overtrumped his partner, missing the grand slam by three tricks. And worst of all, he saw how upset Mikhail Mikhailovich was while he himself did not care. And it was dreadful to think why he did not care.

They could see that he was in pain and said: "We can stop if you're tired. Rest for a while." Rest? Why, he wasn't the least bit tired, they'd finish the rubber. They were all gloomy and silent. Ivan Ilyich knew he was responsible for the gloom that had descended but could do nothing to dispel it. After supper his friends went home, leaving Ivan Ilyich alone with the knowledge that his life had been poisoned and was poisoning the lives of others, and that far from diminishing, that poison was penetrating deeper and deeper into his entire being.

And with this knowledge and the physical pain and the horror as well, he had to go to bed, often to be kept awake by pain the greater part of the night. And the next morning he had to get up again, dress, go to court, talk and write, or if he did not go, put in those twenty-four hours at home, every one of them a torture. And he had to go on living like this, on the brink of disaster, without a single person to understand and pity him.

Chapter 5

One month went by this way, then another. Just before the New Year his brother-in-law came to town and stayed with them. Ivan Ilyich was at court when he arrived. Praskovya Fyodorovna was out shopping. On his return home Ivan Ilyich found his brother-in-law—a robust, ebullient fellow—in the study unpacking his suitcase. The latter raised his head on hearing Ivan Ilyich's step and looked at him for a moment in silence. That look told Ivan Ilyich everything. His brother-in-law opened his mouth to gasp but checked himself. That movement confirmed it all.

"What is it—have I changed?"

"Y-yes . . . you have."

After that, try as he might to steer the conversation back to his appearance, Ivan Ilyich could not get a word out of his brother-in-law. When Praskovya Fyodorovna came back, her brother went in to see her. Ivan Ilyich locked the door of his room and began to examine himself in the mirror—first full face, then in profile. He picked up a photograph he had taken with his wife and compared it to what he saw in the mirror. The change was enormous. Then he bared his arms to the elbow, examined them, pulled down his sleeves, sat down on an ottoman, and fell into a mood blacker than night.

"I mustn't! I mustn't!" he said to himself. He jumped up, went to his desk, opened a case file, started to read but could not go on. He unlocked his door and went into the hall. The door to the drawing room was shut. He tiptoed over and began listening.

"No, you're exaggerating," said Praskovya Fyodorovna.

"Exaggerating? Can't you see for yourself? He's a dead man. Just look at his eyes. Not a spark of life in them. What's wrong with him?"

"No one knows. Nikolaev (another doctor) said something, but I don't understand. Leshchetitsky (the celebrated doctor) said just the opposite."

Ivan Ilyich walked away, went to his room, lay down and began thinking. "A kidney, a floating kidney." He remembered everything the doctors had told him about how the kidney had come loose and was floating about. And by force of imagination he tried to catch that kidney and stop it, to hold it in place. It took so little effort, it seemed. "I'll go and see Pyotr Ivanovich again" (the friend with the doctor friend). He rang, ordered the carriage, and got ready to leave.

"Where are you going, *Jean?*" asked his wife in a particularly sad and unusually kind tone of voice.

This unusual kindness on her part infuriated him. He gave her a somber look.

"I've got to go and see Pyotr Ivanovich."

He went to his friend with the doctor friend and together they went to the doctor. They found him in, and Ivan Ilyich had a long talk with him.

As he went over the anatomical and physiological details of what, in the doctor's view, was going on in him, Ivan Ilyich understood everything.

There was just one thing, a tiny little thing in the caecum. It could be remedied entirely. Just stimulate the energy of one organ, depress the activity of another, then absorption would take place and everything would be fine.

Ivan Ilyich was somewhat late getting home to dinner. He conversed cheerfully after dinner but for some time could not bring himself to go to his room and work. At last he went to his study and immediately set to work. He read through some cases, concentrated, but was constantly aware that he had put off an important, private matter which he would attend to once he was through. When he finished his work he remembered that this private matter involved some thoughts about his caecum. But instead of devoting himself to them he went into the drawing room to have tea. Guests were there talking, playing the piano, and singing; among them was the examining magistrate, a desirable fiancé for their daughter. Ivan Ilyich, as Praskovya Fyodorovna observed, was more cheerful that evening than usual, but never for a moment did he forget that he had put off that important business about his caecum. At eleven o'clock he took leave of everyone and went to his room. Ever since his illness he had slept alone in a little room adjoining his study. He went in, undressed, and picked up a novel by Zola, but instead of reading he lapsed into thought. And in his imagination that longed-for cure of his caecum took place: absorption, evacuation, and a restoration of normal functioning. "Yes, that's the way it works," he told himself. "One need only give nature a hand." He remembered his medicine, raised himself, took it, then lay on his back observing what a beneficial effect the medicine was having, how it was killing the pain. "Only I must take it regularly and avoid anything that could have a bad effect on me. I feel somewhat better already, much better." He began probing his side—it was not painful to the touch. "I really can't feel anything there, it's much better already." He put out the candle and lay on his side—his caecum was improving, absorbing. Suddenly he felt the old, familiar, dull, gnawing pain—quiet, serious, insistent. The same familiar bad taste in his mouth. His heart sank, he felt dazed. "My God, my God!" he muttered. "Again and again, and it will never end." And suddenly he saw things in an entirely different light. "A caecum! A kidney!" he exclaimed inwardly. "It's not a question of a caecum or a kidney, but of life and . . . death. Yes, life was there and now it's going, going, and I can't hold on to it. Yes. Why deceive myself? Isn't it clear to everyone but me that I'm dying, that it's only a question of weeks, days—perhaps minutes? Before there was light, now there is darkness. Before I was here, now I am going there. Where?" He broke out in a cold sweat, his breathing died down. All he could hear was the beating of his heart.

"I'll be gone. What will there be then? Nothing. So where will I be when I'm gone? Can this really be death? No! I don't want this!" He jumped up, wanted to light the candle, groped for it with trembling hands, dropped the candle and candlestick on the floor and sank back on the pillow again. "Why bother? It's all the same," he thought, staring into the darkness with wide-open eyes. "Death. Yes . . . death. And they don't know and don't want to know and have no pity for me. They're playing." (Through the door of his room he caught the distant, intermittent sound of a voice and its accompaniment.) "It's all the same to them, but they'll die too. Fools! I'll go first, then they, but it will be just the same for them. Now they're enjoying themselves, the beasts!" His resentment was choking him. He felt agonizingly, unspeakably miserable. It seemed inconceivable to him that all men invariably had been condemned to suffer this awful horror. He raised himself.

"Something must be wrong. I must calm down, think it all through from the beginning." And he began thinking. "Yes. The beginning of my illness. I banged my side, but I was perfectly all right that day and the next; it hurt a little, then got worse; then came the doctors, then the despondency, the anguish, then more doctors; and all the while I was moving closer and closer to the abyss. Had less and less strength. Kept moving closer and closer. And now I've wasted away, haven't a spark of life in my eyes. It's death, yet I go on thinking about my caecum. I think about how to mend my caecum, whereas this is death. But can it really be death?" Once again he was seized with terror; he gasped for breath, leaned over, began groping for the matches, pressing his elbow for support on the bedside table. It was in his way and it hurt him; he became furious with it, pressed even harder, and knocked it over. And then breathless, in despair, he slumped down on his back, expecting death to strike him that very moment.

Just then the guests were leaving, Praskovya Fyodorovna was seeing them off. Hearing something fall, she came in.

"What is it?"

"Nothing. I accidentally knocked it over."

She went out and came back with a candle. He lay there, breathing heavily and rapidly like a man who has just run a mile, and stared at her with a glazed look.

"What is it, *Jean?*"

"N-nothing. I kn-nocked it over." (What's the point of telling her? She won't understand, he thought.)

And she really did not understand. She picked up the stand, lit the candle for him, and hurried away—she had to see another guest off.

When she returned he was still lying on his back, staring upward.

"What is it? Do you feel worse?"

"Yes."

She shook her head and sat down.

"I wonder, *Jean*, if we shouldn't send for Leshchetitsky."

That meant calling in the celebrated doctor, regardless of the expense. He smiled vindictively and said: "No." She sat there a while longer, then went up and kissed him on the forehead.

As she was kissing him, he hated her with every inch of his being, and he had to restrain himself from pushing her away.

"Good night. God willing, you'll fall asleep."

"Yes."

Chapter 6

Ivan Ilyich saw that he was dying, and he was in a constant state of despair.

In the depth of his heart he knew he was dying, but not only was he unaccustomed to such an idea, he simply could not grasp it, could not grasp it at all.

The syllogism he had learned from Kiesewetter's logic—"Caius is a man, men are mortal, therefore Caius is mortal"—had always seemed to him correct as applied to Caius, but by no means to himself. That man Caius represented man in the abstract, and so the reasoning was perfectly sound; but he was not Caius, not an abstract man; he had always been a creature quite, quite distinct from all the others. He had been little Vanya with a mama and a papa, with Mitya and Volodya, with toys, a coachman, and a nurse, and later with Katenka—Vanya, with all the joys, sorrows, and enthusiasms of his childhood, boyhood, and youth. Had Caius ever known the smell of that little striped leather ball Vanya had loved so much? Had Caius ever kissed his mother's hand so dearly, and had the silk folds of her dress ever rustled so for him? Had Caius ever rioted at school when the pastries were bad? Had he ever been so much in love? Or presided so well over a court session?

Caius really was mortal, and it was only

right that he should die, but for him, Vanya, Ivan Ilyich, with all his thoughts and feelings, it was something else again. And it simply was not possible that he should have to die. That would be too terrible.

So his feelings went.

"If I were destined to die like Caius, I would have known it; an inner voice would have told me. But I was never aware of any such thing; and I and all my friends—we knew our situation was quite different from Caius's. Yet now look what's happened! It can't be. It just can't be, and yet it is. How is it possible? How is one to understand it?"

He could not understand it and tried to dismiss the thought as false, unsound, and morbid, to force it out of his mind with other thoughts that were sound and healthy. But the thought—not just the thought but, it seemed, the reality itself—kept coming back and confronting him.

And one after another, in place of that thought, he called up others, hoping to find support in them. He tried to revert to a way of thinking that had obscured the thought of death from him in the past. But, strangely, everything that had once obscured, hidden, obliterated the awareness of death no longer had that effect. Ivan Ilyich spent most of this latter period trying to recapture habits of feeling that had screened death from him. He would say to himself: "I'll plunge into my work; after all, it was my whole life." And driving his doubts away, he would go to court, enter into conversation with his colleagues and, in his habitually distracted way, take his seat, eyeing the crowd with a pensive look, resting both his emaciated arms on those of his oaken chair, bending over as usual to a colleague, moving the papers over to him, exchanging remarks in a whisper, and then suddenly raising his eyes, holding himself erect, would utter the well-known words that began the proceedings. But suddenly, in the middle of the session, the pain in his side, disregarding the stage the proceedings had reached, would begin its gnawing proceedings. Ivan Ilyich would focus on it, then try to drive the thought of it away, but the pain went right on with its work. And then *It* would come back and stand there and stare at him, and he would be petrified, the light would go out of his eyes, and again he would begin asking himself: "Can *It* alone be true?" And his colleagues and subordinates, amazed and distressed, saw that he who was such a brilliant, subtle judge had become confused, was making mistakes. He would rouse himself, try to regain his composure, somehow bring the session to a close, and return home sadly aware that his judicial work could no longer hide what he wanted it to hide; that his judicial work could not rescue him from *It*. And the worst thing was that *It* drew his attention not so that he would do anything, but merely so that he would look at *It*, look *It* straight in the face and, doing nothing, suffer unspeakable agony.

And to escape from this situation Ivan Ilyich sought relief—other screens—and other screens turned up and for a while seemed to offer some escape; but then they immediately collapsed or

rather became transparent, as though *It* pene-
trated everything and nothing could obscure *It*.

Sometimes during this latter period he went
into the drawing room he had furnished—the
very drawing room where he had fallen, for the
sake of which, he would think with bitter humor,
he had sacrificed his life, for he was certain that
his illness had begun with that injury. He went
in and saw that a deep scratch had cut through
the varnished surface of a table. He tried to find
the cause of the damage and discovered that the
bronze ornament on an album had become bent.
He picked up the album, a costly one that he
had put together with loving care, and became
indignant with his daughter and her friends for
being so careless: in some places the album was
torn, in others the photographs were upside
down. Painstakingly he put everything in order
and bent the ornament back into place.

Later on it would occur to him to transfer
the whole *établissement* with the albums to another corner of the room, next to the plants. He
would call the footman. Either his wife or daughter would come in to help; they would disagree,
contradict one another; he would argue, get angry. But that was all to the good, because it kept
him from thinking about *It*. *It* was nowhere in
sight.

But when he began moving the table himself, his wife said: "Let the servants do it, you'll
only hurt yourself again." And suddenly *It*
flashed through the screen and he saw *It*. *It* had
only appeared as a flash, so he hoped *It* would
disappear, but involuntarily he became aware of

his side: the pain was still there gnawing away at him and he could no longer forget—*It* was staring at him distinctly from behind the plants. What was the point of it all?

"Can it be true that here, on this drapery, as at the storming of a bastion, I lost my life? How awful and how stupid! It just can't be! It can't be, yet it is."

He went to his study, lay down, and once again was left alone with *It*. Face to face with *It*, unable to do anything with *It*. Simply look at *It* and grow numb with horror.

Chapter 7

It is impossible to say how it happened, for it came about gradually, imperceptibly, but in the third month of Ivan Ilyich's illness his wife, his daughter, his son, his acquaintances, the servants, the doctors, and—above all—he himself knew that the only interest he had for others was whether he would soon vacate his place, free the living at last from the constraint of his presence and himself from his sufferings.

He slept less and less. They gave him opium and began morphine injections. But this brought no relief. At first the muffled sense of anguish he experienced in this semiconscious state came as a relief in that it was a new sensation, but then it became as agonizing, if not more so, than the raw pain.

Special foods were prepared for him on the doctors' orders, but these became more and more unpalatable, more and more revolting.

Special arrangements, too, were made for his bowel movements. And this was a regular torture—a torture because of the filth, the unseemliness, the stench, and the knowledge that another person had to assist in this.

Yet it was precisely through this unseemly business that Ivan Ilyich derived some comfort. The pantry boy, Gerasim, always came to carry out the chamber pot. Gerasim was a clean, ruddy-faced young peasant who was thriving on town food. He was always bright and cheerful. At first it embarrassed Ivan Ilyich to see this young fellow in his clean Russian peasant clothes performing such a revolting task.

Once, when he got up from the pot too weak to draw up his trousers, he collapsed into an armchair and, horrified, gazed at his naked thighs with the muscles clearly etched on his wasted flesh. Just then Gerasim entered the room with a light, vigorous step, exuding a pleasant smell of tar from his heavy boots and of fresh winter air. He was wearing a clean hemp apron and a clean cotton shirt with the sleeves rolled up over his strong arms; obviously trying to suppress the joy of life that his face radiated, and thereby not offend the sick man, he avoided looking at Ivan Ilyich and went over to get the pot.

"Gerasim," said Ivan Ilyich in a feeble voice.

Gerasim started, fearing he had done something wrong, and quickly turned his fresh, good-natured, simple, young face, which was showing the first signs of a beard, to the sick man.

"Yes, sir?"

"This must be very unpleasant for you. You must forgive me. I can't help it."

"Oh no, sir!" said Gerasim as he broke into a smile, his eyes and strong white teeth gleaming. "Why shouldn't I help you? You're a sick man."

And with strong, deft hands he performed his usual task, walking out of the room with a light step. Five minutes later, with just as light a step, he returned.

Ivan Ilyich was still sitting in the armchair in the same position.

"Gerasim," he said when the latter had replaced the freshly washed pot. "Please come and help me." Gerasim went over to him. "Lift me up. It's hard for me to get up, and I've sent Dmitry away."

Gerasim took hold of him with his strong arms and with a touch as light as his step, deftly, gently lifted and supported him with one hand, while with the other he pulled up his trousers. He was about to set him down again, but Ivan Ilyich asked that he help him over to the sofa. With no effort and no apparent pressure, Gerasim led—almost carried—him to the sofa and seated him there.

"Thank you. How skillfully . . . how well you do everything."

Gerasim smiled again and turned to leave, but Ivan Ilyich felt so good with him there that he was reluctant to have him go.

"Oh, one thing more. Please move that chair over here. No, the other one, to put under my feet. I feel better with my legs raised."

Gerasim carried the chair over and in one smooth motion set it down gently in place and lifted Ivan Ilyich's legs onto it. It seemed to Ivan Ilyich that he felt better when Gerasim lifted his legs up.

"I feel better with my legs raised," said Ivan Ilyich. "Bring that pillow over and put it under them."

Gerasim did so. He lifted his legs up again and placed the pillow under them. Again Ivan Ilyich felt better while Gerasim raised his legs. When he let them down he seemed to feel worse.

"Gerasim," he said. "Are you busy now?"

"Not at all, sir," said Gerasim, who had learned from the working people in town how to speak to the masters.

"What else do you have to do?"

"What else? I've done everything except chop wood for tomorrow."

"Then could you hold my legs up a bit higher?"

"Why of course I can." Gerasim lifted his legs higher, and it seemed to Ivan Ilyich that in this position he felt no pain at all.

"But what about the firewood?"

"Don't worry yourself about it, sir. I'll get it done."

Ivan Ilyich had Gerasim sit down and hold his legs up, and he began talking to him. And, strangely enough, he thought he felt better while Gerasim was holding his legs.

After that, Ivan Ilyich would send for Gerasim from time to time and have him hold his feet on his shoulders. And he loved to talk to him. Gerasim did everything easily, willingly, simply, and with a goodness of heart that moved Ivan Ilyich. Health, strength, and vitality in other people offended Ivan Ilyich, whereas Gerasim's strength and vitality had a soothing effect on him.

Ivan Ilyich suffered most of all from the lie, the lie which, for some reason, everyone accepted: that he was not dying but was simply ill, and that if he stayed calm and underwent treatment he could expect good results. Yet he knew that regardless of what was done, all he could expect was more agonizing suffering and death. And he was tortured by this lie, tortured by the fact that they refused to acknowledge what he and everyone else knew, that they wanted to lie about his horrible condition and to force him to become a party to that lie. This lie, a lie perpetrated on the eve of his death, a lie that was bound to degrade the awesome, solemn act of his dying to the level of their social calls, their draperies, and the sturgeon they ate for dinner, was an excruciating torture for Ivan Ilyich. And, oddly enough, many times when they were going through their acts with him he came within a hairbreadth of shouting: "Stop your lying! You and I know that I'm dying, so at least stop lying!" But he never had the courage to do it. He saw that the awesome, terrifying act of his dying had been degraded by those about him to the level of a chance unpleasantness, a bit of unseemly behavior (they reacted to him as they would to a man who emitted a foul odor on entering a drawing room); that it had been degraded by that very "propriety" to which he had devoted his entire life. He saw that no one pitied him because no one even cared to understand his situation. Gerasim was the only one who understood and pitied him. And for that reason Ivan Ilyich felt comfortable only with Gerasim. It was a comfort to him when Gerasim sat with him sometimes the whole night through, holding his legs, refusing to go to bed, saying: "Don't worry, Ivan Ilyich, I'll get a good sleep later on"; or when he suddenly addressed him in the familiar form and said: "It would be a different thing if you weren't sick, but as it is, why shouldn't I do a little extra work?" Gerasim was the only one who did not lie; everything he did showed that he alone understood what was happening, saw no need to conceal it, and simply pitied his feeble, wasted master. Once, as Ivan Ilyich was sending him away, he came right out and said: "We all have to die someday, so why shouldn't I help you?" By this he meant that he did not find his work a burden because he was doing it for a dying man, and he hoped that someone would do the same for him when his time came.

In addition to the lie, or owing to it, what tormented Ivan Ilyich most was that no one gave him the kind of compassion he craved. There were moments after long suffering when what he wanted most of all (shameful as it might be for him to admit) was to be pitied like a sick child. He wanted to be caressed, kissed, cried over, as sick children are caressed and comforted. He knew that he was an important functionary with a graying beard, and so this was impossible; yet all the same he longed for it. There was something approaching this in his relationship with Gerasim, and so the relationship was a comfort to him. Ivan Ilyich wanted to cry, wanted to be caressed and cried over, yet his colleague Shebek, a member of the court, would come, and instead of crying and getting some affection, Ivan Ilyich would assume a serious, stern, profound expression and, by force of habit, offer his opinion about a decision by the Court of Appeals and stubbornly defend it. Nothing did so much to poison the last days of Ivan Ilyich's life as this falseness in himself and in those around him.

Chapter 8

It was morning. He knew it was morning simply because Gerasim had gone and Pyotr, the footman, had come, snuffed out the candles, drawn back one of the curtains, and quietly begun to tidy up the room. Morning or night, Friday or Sunday, made no difference, everything was the same: that gnawing, excruciating, incessant pain; that awareness of life irrevocably passing but not yet gone; that dreadful, loathsome death, the only reality, relentlessly closing in on him; and that same endless lie. What did days, weeks, or hours matter?

"Will you have tea, sir?"

"He wants order, so the masters should drink tea in the morning," thought Ivan Ilyich. But he merely replied: "No."

"Would you care to move to the sofa, sir?"

"He wants to tidy up the room and I'm in the way. I represent filth and disorder," thought Ivan Ilyich. But he merely replied: "No, leave me alone."

The footman busied himself a while longer. Ivan Ilyich stretched out his hand. Pyotr went up to him obligingly.

"What would you like, sir?"

"My watch."

Pyotr picked up the watch, which was lying within Ivan Ilyich's reach, and gave it to him.

"Half-past eight. Are they up?"

"No, sir. Vasily Ivanovich (the son) went to school and Praskovya Fyodorovna left orders to awaken her if you asked. Shall J, sir?"

"No, don't bother," he said. "Perhaps I should have some tea," he thought, and said: "Yes, tea . . . bring me some."

Pyotr headed for the door. Ivan Ilyich was terrified at the thought of being left alone. "What can I do to keep him here?" he thought. "Oh, of course, the medicine."

"Pyotr, give me my medicine," he said. "Why not?" he thought. "Maybe the medicine will still do some good." He took a spoonful and swallowed it. "No, it won't help. It's just nonsense, a hoax," he decided as soon as he felt that familiar, sickly, hopeless taste in his mouth. "No, I can't believe in it anymore. But why this pain, this pain? If only it would let up for a minute!" He began to moan. Pyotr came back.

"No, go. Bring me some tea."

Pyotr went out. Left alone Ivan Ilyich moaned less from the pain, agonizing as it was, than from anguish. "The same thing, on and on, the same endless days and nights. If only it would come quicker! If only *what* would come quicker? Death, darkness. No! No! Anything is better than death!"

When Pyotr returned with the tea, Ivan Ilyich looked at him in bewilderment for some time, unable to grasp who and what he was. Pyotr was disconcerted by that look. Seeing his confusion, Ivan Ilyich came to his senses.

"Yes," he said. "Tea . . . good. Put it down.

Only help me wash up and put on a clean shirt."

And Ivan Ilyich began to wash himself. Pausing now and then to rest, he washed his hands and face, brushed his teeth, combed his hair, and looked in the mirror. He was horrified, particularly horrified to see the limp way his hair clung to his pale brow. He knew he would be even more horrified by the sight of his body, and so while his shirt was being changed he avoided looking at it. Finally it was all over. He put on a dressing gown, wrapped himself in a plaid, and sat down in an armchair to have his tea. For a brief moment he felt refreshed, but as soon as he began to drink his tea he sensed that same taste again, that same pain. He forced himself to finish the tea and then lay down, stretched out his legs, and sent Pyotr away.

The same thing again and again. One moment a spark of hope gleams, the next a sea of despair rages; and always the pain, the pain, always the anguish, the same thing on and on. Left alone he feels horribly depressed, wants to call someone, but knows beforehand that with others present it will be even worse. "Oh, for some morphine again—to sink into oblivion. I'll tell the doctor he must think of something to give me."

One hour then another pass this way. Then there is a ring in the entranceway. The doctor perhaps? The doctor indeed—fresh, hearty, stocky, cheerful, and with a look on his face that seems to say: "Now, now, you've had yourself a bad scare, but we're going to fix everything right away." The doctor knows this expression

109

is inappropriate here, but he has put it on once and for all and can't take it off—like a man who has donned a frock coat in the morning to make a round of social calls.

The doctor rubs his hands briskly, reassuringly. "I'm chilled. Freezing cold outside. Just give me a minute to warm up," he says in a tone implying that one need only wait a moment until he warmed up and he would set everything right.

"Well, now, how are you?"

Ivan Ilyich feels the doctor wants to say: "How goes it?" but that even he knows this won't do, and so he says: "What sort of night did you have?"

Ivan Ilyich looks at the doctor inquisitively as if to say: "Won't you ever be ashamed of your lying?" But the doctor does not wish to understand such a question.

"Terrible. Just like all the others," Ivan Ilyich said. "The pain never leaves, never subsides. If only you'd give me something!"

"Yes, you sick people are always carrying on like this. Well, now, I seem to have warmed up. Even Praskovya Fyodorovna, who's so exacting, couldn't find fault with my temperature. Well, now I can say good morning." And the doctor shakes his hand.

Then, dispensing with all the banter, the doctor assumes a serious air and begins to examine the patient, taking his pulse, his temperature, sounding his chest, listening to his heart and lungs.

Ivan Ilyich knows for certain, beyond any doubt, that this is all nonsense, sheer deception, but when the doctor gets down on his knees, bends over him, placing his ear higher, then lower, and with the gravest expression on his face goes through all sorts of contortions, Ivan Ilyich is taken in by it, just as he used to be taken in by the speeches of lawyers, even though he knew perfectly well they were lying and why they were lying.

The doctor is still kneeling on the sofa, tapping away at him, when there is a rustle of silk at the doorway and Praskovya Fyodorovna can be heard reproaching Pyotr for not informing her of the doctor's arrival.

She comes in, kisses her husband, and at once tries to demonstrate that she has been up for some time, and owing simply to a misunderstanding failed to be in the room when the doctor arrived.

Ivan Ilyich looks her over from head to toe and resents her for the whiteness, plumpness, and cleanliness of her arms and neck, the luster of her hair, and the spark of vitality that gleams in her eyes. He hates her with every inch of his being. And her touch causes an agonizing well of hatred to surge up in him.

Her attitude toward him and his illness is the same as ever. Just as the doctor had adopted a certain attitude toward his patients, which he could not change, so she had adopted one toward him: that he was not doing what he should and was himself to blame, and she could only reproach him tenderly for this. And she could no longer change this attitude.

"He just doesn't listen, you know. He

doesn't take his medicine on time. And worst of all, he lies in a position that is surely bad for him—with his legs up."

And she told him how he made Gerasim hold his legs up.

The doctor smiled disdainfully, indulgently, as if to say: "What can you do? Patients sometimes get absurd ideas into their heads, but we have to forgive them."

When he had finished his examination the doctor glanced at his watch, and then Praskovya Fyodorovna announced to Ivan Ilyich that whether he liked it or not, she had called in a celebrated physician, and that he and Mikhail Danilovich (the regular doctor) would examine him together that day and discuss his case.

"So no arguments, please. I'm doing this for my sake," she said ironically, letting him know that she was doing it all for his sake and had said this merely to deny him the right to protest. He scowled and said nothing. He felt that he was trapped in such a mesh of lies that it was difficult to make sense out of anything.

Everything she did for him was done strictly for her sake; and she told him she was doing for her sake what she actually was, making this seem so incredible that he was bound to take it to mean just the reverse.

At half-past eleven the celebrated doctor did indeed arrive. Again there were soundings and impressive talk in his presence and in the next room about the kidney and the caecum, and questions and answers exchanged with such an air of importance that once again, instead of the real question of life and death, the only one confronting Ivan Ilyich, the question that had arisen concerned a kidney or a caecum that was not behaving properly, and that would soon get a good trouncing from Mikhail Danilovich and the celebrity and be forced to mend its ways.

The celebrated doctor took leave of him with a grave but not hopeless air. And when Ivan Ilyich looked up at him, his eyes glistening with hope and fear, and timidly asked whether there was any chance of recovery, he replied that he could not vouch for it but there was a chance. The look of hope Ivan Ilyich gave the doctor as he watched him leave was so pathetic that, seeing it, Praskovya Fyodorovna actually burst into tears as she left the study to give the celebrated doctor his fee.

The improvement in his morale prompted by the doctor's encouraging remarks did not last long. Once again the same room, the same pictures, draperies, wallpaper, medicine bottles, and the same aching, suffering body. Ivan Ilyich began to moan. They gave him an injection and he lost consciousness.

When he came to, it was twilight; his dinner was brought in. He struggled to get down some broth. Then everything was the same again, and again night was coming on.

After dinner, at seven o'clock, Praskovya Fyodorovna came into his room in evening dress, her full bosom drawn up tightly by her corset, and traces of powder showing on her face. She had reminded him in the morning that they were going to the theater. Sarah Bernhardt had come to town, and at his insistence they had reserved a box. He had forgotten about this and was hurt by the sight of her elaborate attire. But he concealed his indignation when he remembered that he himself had urged them to reserve a box and go, because the aesthetic enjoyment would be edifying for the children.

Praskovya Fyodorovna had come in looking self-satisfied but guilty. She sat down and asked how he was feeling—merely for the sake of asking, as he could see, not because she wanted to find out anything, for she knew there was nothing to find out; and she went on to say what she felt was necessary: that under no circumstances would she have gone except that the box was reserved, and that Helene and their daughter and Petrishchev (the examining magistrate, their daughter's fiancé) were going, and it was unthinkable to let them go alone, but that she would much prefer to sit home with him, and would he promise to follow the doctor's orders while she was away.

"Oh, and Fyodor Petrovich (the fiancé) would like to come in. May he? And Liza?"

"All right."

His daughter came in all decked out in a gown that left much of her young flesh exposed; she was making a show of that very flesh which, for him, was the cause of so much agony. Strong, healthy, and obviously in love, she was impatient with illness, suffering, and death, which interfered with her happiness.

Fyodor Petrovich came in, too, in evening dress, his hair curled *à la Capoul*, a stiff white collar encircling his long, sinewy neck, an enormous white shirtfront over his chest, narrow black trousers hugging his strong thighs, a white glove drawn tightly over one hand, an opera hat clasped in the other.

Behind him the schoolboy son crept in unnoticed, all decked out in a new uniform, poor fellow, with gloves on and those awful dark circles under his eyes, whose meaning Ivan Ilyich understood only too well. He had always felt sorry for his son. And he found the boy's frightened, pitying look terrifying to behold. It seemed to Ivan Ilyich that, except for Gerasim, Vasya was the only one who understood and pitied him.

They all sat down and again asked how he was feeling. Then silence. Liza asked her mother about the opera glasses. This led to an argument between mother and daughter about who had mislaid them. It occasioned some unpleasantness.

Fyodor Petrovich asked Ivan Ilyich if he had ever seen Sarah Bernhardt. Ivan Ilyich did not understand the question at first, but then he said: "No, have you?"

"Yes, in *Adrienne Lecouvreur*."

Praskovya Fyodorovna said she had been particularly good in something or other. The daughter disagreed. They started a conversation about the charm and naturalness of her acting—precisely the kind of conversation people always have on the subject.

In the middle of the conversation Fyodor Petrovich glanced at Ivan Ilyich and stopped talking. The others also looked at him and stopped talking. Ivan Ilyich was staring straight ahead with glittering eyes, obviously infuriated with them. The situation had to be rectified, but there was no way to rectify it. The silence had to be broken. No one ventured to break it, and they began to fear that the lie dictated by propriety suddenly would be exposed and the truth become clear to all. Liza was the first who ventured to break the silence. She wanted to conceal what they were feeling but, in going too far, she divulged it.

"Well, *if we're going*, it's time we left," she said, glancing at her watch, a gift from her father. And smiling at her young man in a significant but barely perceptible way about something only they understood, she stood up, rustling her dress.

They all got up, said goodbye, and left.

When they had gone, Ivan Ilyich thought he felt better: the lie was gone—it had left with them. But the pain remained. That same pain, that same fear that made nothing harder, nothing easier. Everything was getting worse.

Again time dragged on, minute by minute, hour by hour, on and on without end, with the inevitable end becoming more and more horrifying.

"Yes, send Gerasim," he said in reply to a question Pyotr asked him.

Chapter 9

His wife returned late that night. She tiptoed into the room, but he heard her; he opened
his eyes and quickly closed them again. She
wanted to send Gerasim away and sit with him
herself, but he opened his eyes and said:

"No, go away."

"Are you in very great pain?"

"It doesn't matter."

"Take some opium."

He consented and drank some. She went
away.

Until about three in the morning he was in
an agonizing delirium. It seemed to him that he
and his pain were being thrust into a narrow
black sack—a deep one—were thrust farther and
farther in but could not be pushed to the bottom.
And this dreadful business was causing him suffering. He was afraid of that sack, yet wanted
to fall through; struggled, yet cooperated. And
then suddenly he lost his grip and fell—and re-
gained consciousness. Gerasim was still sitting
at the foot of the bed, dozing quietly, patiently,
while Ivan Ilyich lay with his emaciated, stock-
inged feet on his shoulders. The same shaded
candle was there and the same incessant pain.

"Go, Gerasim," he whispered.

"It's all right, sir. I'll stay awhile."

"No, go."

He lowered his legs, turned sideways with

his arm nestled under his cheek, and began to feel terribly sorry for himself. He waited until Gerasim had gone into the next room, and then, no longer able to restrain himself, cried like a baby. He cried about his helplessness, about his terrible loneliness, about the cruelty of people, about the cruelty of God, about the absence of God.

"Why hast Thou done all this? Why hast Thou brought me to this? Why dost Thou torture me so? For what?"

He did not expect an answer, and he cried because there was no answer and there could be none. The pain started up again, but he did not stir, did not call out. He said to himself: "Go on then! Hit me again! But what for? What for? What have I done to Thee?"

Then he quieted down and not only stopped crying but held his breath and became all attention: he seemed to be listening—not to an audible voice, but to the voice of his soul, to the flow of thoughts surging within him.

"What do you want?" was the first thought sufficiently intelligible to be expressed in words. "What do you want? What do you want?" he repeated inwardly. "What? Not to suffer. To live," he replied.

And once again he listened with such rapt attention that even the pain did not distract him.

"To live? How?" asked the voice of his soul.

"Why, to live as I did before—happily and pleasantly."

"As you lived before, happily and pleasantly?" asked the voice.

And in his imagination he called to mind the best moments of his pleasant life. Yet, strangely enough, all the best moments of his pleasant life now seemed entirely different than they had in the past—all except the earliest memories of childhood. Way back in his childhood there had been something really pleasant, something he could live with were it ever to recur. But the person who had experienced that happiness no longer existed. It was as though he were recalling the memories of another man.

As soon as he got to the period that had produced the present Ivan Ilyich, all the seeming joys of his life vanished before his sight and turned into something trivial and often nasty.

And the farther he moved from childhood, the closer he came to the present, the more trivial and questionable these joyful experiences appeared. Beginning with the years he had spent in law school. A little of what was genuinely good had still existed then: there had been playfulness and friendship and hope. But by the time he reached the upper classes, the good moments in his life had become rarer. After that, during the period he worked for the governor, there had also been some good moments—memories of his love for a woman. But then everything became more and more mixed, and less of what was good remained. Later on there was even less, and the farther he went, the less there was.

His marriage—a mere accident—and his disillusionment with it, and his wife's bad breath, and the sensuality, and the pretense! And that deadly service, and those worries about money; and so it had gone for a year, two years, ten years, twenty years—on and on in the same way. And the longer it lasted, the more deadly it became. "It's as though I had been going steadily downhill while I imagined I was going up. That's exactly what happened. In public opinion I was moving uphill, but to the same extent life was slipping away from me. And now it's gone and all I can do is die!

"What does it all mean? Why has it happened? It's inconceivable, inconceivable that life was so senseless and disgusting. And if it really was so disgusting and senseless, why should I have to die, and die in agony? Something must be wrong. Perhaps I did not live as I should have," it suddenly occurred to him. "But how could that be when I did everything one is supposed to?" he replied and immediately dismissed the one solution to the whole enigma of life and death, considering it utterly impossible.

"Then what do you want now? To live? Live how? Live as you did in court when the usher proclaimed: 'The court is open!' The court is open, open," he repeated inwardly. "Now comes the judgment! But I'm not guilty!" he cried out indignantly. "What is this for?" And he stopped crying and, turning his face to the wall, began to dwell on one and the same question: "Why all this horror? What is it for?"

But think as he might, he could find no answer. And when it occurred to him, as it often did, that he had not lived as he should have, he immediately recalled how correct his whole life had been and dismissed this bizarre idea.

Chapter 10

Another two weeks passed. Ivan Ilyich no longer got off the sofa. He did not want to lie in bed and so he lay on the sofa. And as he lay there, facing the wall most of the time, he suffered, all alone, the same inexplicable suffering and, all alone, brooded on the same inexplicable question: "What is this? Is it true that this is death?" And an inner voice answered: "Yes, it is true." "Then why these torments?" And the voice answered: "For no reason—they just are." Above and beyond this there was nothing.

From the start of his illness, from the time he first went to a doctor, Ivan Ilyich's life had been divided into two contradictory and fluctuating moods: one a mood of despair and expectation of an incomprehensible and terrible death; the other a mood of hope filled with intent observation of the course of his bodily functions. At times he was confronted with nothing but a kidney or an intestine that was temporarily evading its duty; at others nothing but an unfathomable, horrifying death from which there was no escape.

These two moods had fluctuated since the onset of his illness, but the farther that illness progressed, the more unlikely and preposterous considerations about his kidney became and the more real his sense of impending death.

He had merely to recall what he had been like three months earlier and what he was now, to remember how steadily he had gone downhill, for all possibility of hope to be shattered.

During the last days of the isolation in which he lived, lying on the sofa with his face to the wall, isolation in the midst of a populous city among numerous friends and relatives, an isolation that could not have been greater anywhere, either in the depths of the sea or the bowels of the earth—during the last days of that terrible isolation, Ivan Ilyich lived only with memories of the past. One after another images of his past came to mind. His recollections always began with what was closest in time and shifted back to what was most remote, to his childhood, and lingered there. If he thought of the stewed prunes he had been served that day, he remembered the raw, shrivelled French prunes he had eaten as a child, the special taste they had, the way his mouth watered when he got down to the pit; and along with the memory of that taste came a whole series of memories of those days: of his nurse, his brother, his toys. "I mustn't think about them—it's too painful," he would tell himself and shift back to the present. He would look at the button on the back of the sofa and the crease in the morocco. "Morocco is expensive, doesn't wear well; we had a quarrel over it. But there had been another morocco and another quarrel—the time we tore papa's briefcase and got punished, but mama brought us some tarts." And again his memories centered on his childhood, and again he found them painful and tried to drive them away by thinking about something else.

And together with this train of recollections, another flashed through his mind—recollections of how his illness had progressed and become more acute. Here, too, the farther back in time he went, the more life he found. There had been more goodness in his life earlier and more of life itself. And the one fused with the other. "Just as my torments are getting worse and worse, so my whole life got worse and worse," he thought. There was only one bright spot back at the beginning of life; after that things grew blacker and blacker, moved faster and faster. "In inverse ratio to the square of the distance from death," thought Ivan Ilyich. And the image of a stone hurtling downward with increasing velocity became fixed in his mind. Life, a series of increasing sufferings, falls faster and faster toward its end—the most frightful suffering. "I am falling . . ." He shuddered, shifted back and forth, wanted to resist, but by then knew there was no resisting. And again, weary of contemplating but unable to tear his eyes away from what was right there before him, he stared at the back of the sofa and waited—waited for that dreadful fall, shock, destruction. "Resistance is impossible," he said to himself. "But if only I could understand the reason for this agony. Yet even that is impossible. It would make sense if one could say I had not lived as I should have. But such an admission is impossible," he uttered inwardly, remembering how his life had conformed to all the laws, rules, and proprieties. "That is a point I cannot grant," he told himself, smiling ironically, as though someone could see that smile of his and be taken in by it. "There is no explanation. Agony. Death. Why?"

Chapter 11

Two more weeks went by this way. During that time the event Ivan Ilyich and his wife had hoped for occurred: Petrishchev made a formal proposal. It happened in the evening. The next day Praskovya Fyodorovna went into her husband's room thinking over how she would announce the proposal, but during the night Ivan Ilyich had undergone a change for the worse. Praskovya Fyodorovna found him on the same sofa but in a different position. He was lying flat on his back, moaning, and staring straight ahead with a fixed look in his eyes.

She started to say something about his medicine. He shifted his gaze to her. So great was the animosity in that look—animosity toward her—that she broke off without finishing what she had to say.

"For Christ's sake, let me die in peace!" he said.

She wanted to leave, but at that moment their daughter came in and went over to say good morning to him. He looked at her as he had at his wife, and when she asked how he was feeling coldly replied that they would soon be rid of him. Both of them were silent, sat there for a while, and then went away.

"Is it our fault?" Liza asked her mother.

125

"You'd think we were to blame. I'm sorry for papa, but why should he torture us like this?"

The doctor came at his usual time. Ivan Ilyich merely answered Yes or No to his questions, glowered at him throughout the visit, and toward the end said:

"You know perfectly well you can do nothing to help me, so leave me alone."

"We can ease your suffering," said the doctor.

"You can't even do that; leave me alone."

The doctor went into the drawing room and told Praskovya Fyodorovna that his condition was very bad and that only one remedy, opium, could relieve his pain, which must be excruciating.

The doctor said his physical agony was dreadful, and that was true; but even more dreadful was his moral agony, and it was this that tormented him most.

What had induced his moral agony was that during the night, as he gazed at Gerasim's broadboned, sleepy, good-natured face, he suddenly asked himself: "What if my entire life, my entire conscious life, simply was *not the real thing*?"

It occurred to him that what had seemed utterly inconceivable before—that he had not lived the kind of life he should have—might in fact be true. It occurred to him that those scarcely perceptible impulses of his to protest what people of high rank considered good, vague impulses which he had always suppressed, might have been precisely what mattered, and all the rest not been the real thing. His official duties, his manner of life, his family, the values adhered to by people in society and in his profession—all these might not have been the real thing. He tried to come up with a defense of these things and suddenly became aware of the insubstantiality of them all. And there was nothing left to defend.

"But if that is the case," he asked himself, "and I am taking leave of life with the awareness that I squandered all I was given and have no possibility of rectifying matters—what then?" He lay on his back and began to review his whole life in an entirely different light.

When, in the morning, he saw first the footman, then his wife, then his daughter, and then the doctor, their every gesture, their every word, confirmed the horrible truth revealed to him during the night. In them he saw himself, all he had lived by, saw clearly that all this was not the real thing but a dreadful, enormous deception that shut out both life and death. This awareness intensified his physical sufferings, magnified them tenfold. He moaned and tossed and clutched at his bedclothes. He felt they were choking and suffocating him, and he hated them on that account.

He was given a large dose of opium and lost consciousness, but at dinnertime it all started again. He drove everyone away and tossed from side to side.

His wife came to him and said:

"*Jean*, dear, do this for me." (For me?)

"It can't do you any harm, and it often helps. Really, it's such a small thing. And even healthy people often . . ."

He opened his eyes wide.

"What? Take the sacrament? Why? I don't want to! And yet . . ."

She began to cry.

"Then you will, dear? I'll send for our priest, he's such a nice man."

"Fine, very good," he said.

When the priest came and heard his confession, he relented, seemed to feel relieved of his doubts and therefore of his agony, and experienced a brief moment of hope. Again he began to think about his caecum and the possibility of curing it. As he took the sacrament, there were tears in his eyes.

When they laid him down afterward, he felt better for a second and again held out hope of living. He began to think of the operation the doctors had proposed doing. "I want to live, to live!" he said to himself. His wife came in to congratulate him on taking the sacrament; she said the things people usually do, and then added:

"You really do feel better, don't you?"

"Yes," he said without looking at her.

Her clothes, her figure, the expression of her face, the sound of her voice—all these said to him: "*Not the real thing*. Everything you lived by and still live by is a lie, a deception that blinds you from the reality of life and death." And no sooner had he thought this than hatred welled up in him, and with the hatred, excruciating physical pain, and with the pain, an awareness of inevitable, imminent destruction. The pain took a new turn: it began to grind and shoot and constrict his breathing.

The expression on his face when he uttered that "Yes" was dreadful. Having uttered it, he looked his wife straight in the eye, and with a rapidity extraordinary for one so weak, flung himself face downward and shouted:

"Go away! Go away! Leave me alone!"

Chapter 12

That moment started three days of incessant
screaming, screaming so terrible that even two
rooms away one could not hear it without trembling. The moment he had answered his wife,
he realized that he was lost, that there was no
return, that the end had come, the very end, and
that his doubts, still unresolved, remained with
him.

"Oh! Oh! No!" he screamed in varying
tones. He had begun by shouting: "I don't want
it! I don't!" and went on uttering screams with
that "O" sound.

For three straight days, during which time
ceased to exist for him, he struggled desperately
in that black sack into which an unseen, invin-
cible force was thrusting him. He struggled as
a man condemned to death struggles in the hands
of an executioner, knowing there is no escape.
And he felt that with every minute, despite his
efforts to resist, he was coming closer and closer
to what terrified him. He felt he was in agony
because he was being shoved into that black hole,
but even more because he was unable to get right
into it. What prevented him from getting into
it was the belief that his life had been a good
one. This justification of his life held him fast,
kept him from moving forward, and caused him
more agony than anything else.

Suddenly some force struck him in the chest and the side and made his breathing even more constricted: he plunged into the hole and there at the bottom, something was shining. What had happened to him was what one frequently experiences in a railway car when one thinks one is going forward but is actually moving backward, and suddenly becomes aware of the actual direction.

"Yes, all of it was simply *not the real thing*. But no matter. I can still make it *the real thing*— I can. But what *is* the real thing?" Ivan Ilyich asked himself and suddenly grew quiet.

This took place at the end of the third day, an hour before his death. Just then his son crept quietly into the room and went up to his bed. The dying man was still screaming desperately and flailing his arms. One hand fell on the boy's head. The boy grasped it, pressed it to his lips, and began to cry. At that very moment Ivan Ilyich fell through and saw a light, and it was revealed to him that his life had not been what it should have but that he could still rectify the situation. "But what *is* the real thing?" he asked himself and grew quiet, listening. Just then he felt someone kissing his hand. He opened his eyes and looked at his son. He grieved for him. His wife came in and went up to him. He looked at her. She gazed at him with an open mouth, with unwiped tears on her nose and cheeks, with a look of despair on her face. He grieved for her.

"Yes, I'm torturing them," he thought. "They feel sorry for me, but it will be better for them when I die." He wanted to tell them this but lacked the strength to speak. "But why speak—I must do something," he thought. He looked at his wife and, indicating his son with a glance, said:

"Take him away . . . sorry for him . . . and you." He wanted to add: "Forgive" but instead said "Forget," and too feeble to correct himself, dismissed it, knowing that He who needed to understand would understand.

And suddenly it became clear to him that what had been oppressing him and would not leave him suddenly was vanishing all at once—from two sides, ten sides, all sides. He felt sorry for them, he had to do something to keep from hurting them. To deliver them and himself from this suffering. "How good and how simple!" he thought. "And the pain?" he asked himself. "Where has it gone? Now, then, pain, where are you?"

He waited for it attentively.

"Ah, there it is. Well, what of it? Let it be."

"And death? Where is it?"

He searched for his accustomed fear of death and could not find it. Where was death? What death? There was no fear because there was no death.

Instead of death there was light.

"So that's it!" he exclaimed. "What bliss!"

All this happened in a single moment, but the significance of that moment was lasting. For those present, his agony continued for another two hours. Something rattled in his chest; his emaciated body twitched. Then the rattling and wheezing gradually diminished.

"It is all over," said someone standing beside him.

He heard these words and repeated them in his soul.

"Death is over," he said to himself. "There is no more death."

He drew in a breath, broke off in the middle of it, stretched himself out, and died.

THE BANTAM SHAKESPEARE COLLECTION

The Complete Works in 28 Volumes

Edited with Introductions by David Bevington

Forewords by Joseph Papp

<table>
<tr><td>___ANTONY AND</td><td></td><td></td></tr>
<tr><td>CLEOPATRA</td><td>21289-3</td><td>$3.95</td></tr>
<tr><td>___AS YOU LIKE IT</td><td>21290-7</td><td>$3.95</td></tr>
<tr><td>___A COMEDY</td><td></td><td></td></tr>
<tr><td>OF ERRORS</td><td>21291-5</td><td>$3.95</td></tr>
<tr><td>___HAMLET</td><td>21292-3</td><td>$3.95</td></tr>
<tr><td>___HENRY IV, PART I</td><td>21293-1</td><td>$3.95</td></tr>
<tr><td>___HENRY IV, PART II</td><td>21294-X</td><td>$3.95</td></tr>
<tr><td>___HENRY V</td><td>21295-8</td><td>$3.95</td></tr>
<tr><td>___JULIUS CAESAR</td><td>21296-6</td><td>$3.95</td></tr>
<tr><td>___KING LEAR</td><td>21297-4</td><td>$3.95</td></tr>
<tr><td>___MACBETH</td><td>21298-2</td><td>$3.95</td></tr>
<tr><td>___THE MERCHANT</td><td></td><td></td></tr>
<tr><td>OF VENICE</td><td>21299-0</td><td>$2.95</td></tr>
<tr><td>___A MIDSUMMER NIGHT'S</td><td></td><td></td></tr>
<tr><td>DREAM</td><td>21300-8</td><td>$3.95</td></tr>
<tr><td>___MUCH ADO ABOUT</td><td></td><td></td></tr>
<tr><td>NOTHING</td><td>21301-6</td><td>$3.95</td></tr>
<tr><td>___OTHELLO</td><td>21302-4</td><td>$3.95</td></tr>
<tr><td>___RICHARD II</td><td>21303-2</td><td>$3.95</td></tr>
<tr><td>___RICHARD III</td><td>21304-0</td><td>$3.95</td></tr>
<tr><td>___ROMEO AND</td><td></td><td></td></tr>
<tr><td>JULIET</td><td>21305-9</td><td>$3.95</td></tr>
<tr><td>___THE TAMING OF</td><td></td><td></td></tr>
<tr><td>THE SHREW</td><td>21306-7</td><td>$3.95</td></tr>
<tr><td>___THE TEMPEST</td><td>21307-5</td><td>$3.95</td></tr>
<tr><td>___TWELFTH NIGHT</td><td>21308-3</td><td>$3.50</td></tr>
</table>

___FOUR COMEDIES (*The Taming of the Shrew, A Midsummer Night's Dream, The Merchant of Venice,* and *Twelfth Night*) 21281-8 $4.95

___THREE EARLY COMEDIES (*Love's Labor's Lost, The Two Gentlemen of Verona,* and *The Merry Wives of Windsor*) 21282-6 $4.95

___FOUR TRAGEDIES (*Hamlet, Othello, King Lear,* and *Macbeth*) 21283-4 $5.95

___HENRY VI, PARTS I, II, and III 21285-0 $4.95

___KING JOHN and IIHENRY VIII 21286-9 $4.95

___MEASURE FOR MEASURE, ALL'S WELL THAT ENDS WELL, and TROILUS AND CRESSIDA 21287-7 $4.95

___THE LATE ROMANCES (*Pericles, Cymbeline, The Winter's Tale,* and *The Tempest*) 21288-5 $4.95

___THE POEMS 21309-1 $4.95

Ask for these books at your local bookstore or use this page to order.

Please send me the books I have checked above. I am enclosing $____ (add $2.50 to cover postage and handling). Send check or money order, no cash or C.O.D.'s, please.

Name _____

Address _____

City/State/Zip _____

Send order to: Bantam Books, Dept. SH 2, 2451 S. Wolf Rd., Des Plaines, IL 60018
Allow four to six weeks for delivery.
Prices and availability subject to change without notice.   SH 2 3/96

Discover the world of

LOUISA MAY ALCOTT

Little Women
_____ 21275-3 $3.95/$4.95

Little Women is one of the best-loved books of all time. Lovely Meg, talented Jo, frail Beth, spoiled Amy: these are the four March sisters, who learn the hard lessons of poverty and of growing up in New England during the Civil War.

Jo's Boys
_____ 21449-7 $3.50/$4.50

Louisa May Alcott continues the story of her feisty protagonist Jo in this final novel chronicling the adventures and the misadventures of the March family.